Reign

The Assault of Lucifer Morningstar

The Silver Blood Knight Series

(Book 1)

CAROL MCKIBBEN

www.trollriverpub.com

REIGN: The Assault of Lucifer Morningstar
The Silver Blood Knight (Book 1)
Copyright © 2020 Carol McKiben
ISBN: 978-1-946454-76-8

Join the fun with Author Carol McKibben for giveaways, updates and new release opportunities at: http://eepurl.com/bAuq2b

Other books by Carol McKibben:

<u>The Snow Blood series:</u>

Snow Blood: Season 1

Snow Blood Season 2

Snow Blood: Season 3

Snow Blood: Season 4

Snow Blood: Season 5

Kane: The First Blood Son (prequel of the Snow Blood series)

<u>The First Blood Son series:</u>

Moon Blood: The First Blood Son series (Book 1)

Moon Blood: The First Blood Son series (Book 2)

Moon Blood: The First Blood Son series (Book 3)

Moon Blood: The First Blood Son series (Book 4)

Moon Blood: The First Blood Son series (Book 5)

<u>Stand alone novels:</u>

Riding Through It

Luke's Tale

Contents

DEDICATION

For Lee Brown and Franny Jaynes because they have always supported my writing. I love them very much.

PROLOGUE

GAMINO AND LUCIFER

Vito Gamino raged against the world. The head of the Italian Mafia sat in his palatial estate in Sicily drunk with grief.

Tears streaming from his eyes, he raised his hefty body from his gold brocade chair, picked up a Waterford Marquis crystal glass, and pitched it into the marble fireplace of his den. "Damn God!"

Three years had passed since he had lost his entire family—his wife and two young sons—to the zombie plague while they were visiting Florence. Yet, his anger and grief weighed on him like a heavy blanket he couldn't shed.

"What kind of God would turn an entire city into a herd of zombies? Why had I let Marina and the boys go alone?"

Gamino's mafioso family had at first thought he'd married the young, beautiful model out of ego. They had wondered how she could possibly have been attracted to the stubby, balding mob boss, except for the money and power it brought. They had soon realized, however, that this odd couple truly adored each other.

Gamino whirled around, picked up another expensive glass, and hurled it into the fireplace.

His servants and henchmen, afraid to be in his presence when he was in one of his frequent dark moods, hovered outside the door.

"Damn God! Damn humanity!" He launched an entire crystal decanter filled with Loch Ness Blended Whisky into the fireplace which shot out flames upon contact.

"Yes, let's do so." A deep, sinister voice spoke behind Gamino, who whirled in surprise.

His intoxication flooded away at the sight in front of him.

The man was beautiful. The strong facial structure framed by long golden hair enhanced the bluest eyes the mobster had ever seen. They gleamed with cold malice.

Gamino stepped back, almost losing his balance. "Who? What? How did you get in here?"

At his question, the henchmen outside his door attempted to enter only to be pushed back with a wave of the beautiful one's hand. The door they'd tried to open slammed back into them. Their bodies, along with that of the servants, fell and they were dead before they hit the floor.

The full lips in the handsome face smiled at the gangster. "I think you know."

"No, no, I don't. Satan wouldn't be beautiful."

Satan suddenly transformed into a menacing horned creature with scaly red skin, a sharp, pointed tail, long claws, and yellow catlike eyes.

Gamino rushed toward the den's double doors when the man's words froze him.

"What is it you desire most in this world, Gamino?" Just as quickly, the intruder reverted to his handsome demeanor. "Your lost family, perhaps? What if I told you I could restore them to you?"

The mob boss whirled around, his eyebrows raised. "What? You couldn't do that."

Lucifer Morningstar smirked. "Of course, I could. I'm the one that took them from you. Didn't you know?"

Gamino clenched his fists, let out a growl resembling one of a hurt animal, and charged, stumbling toward the devil. "Damn you!"

Lucifer halted the man in his tracks with a flick of his wrist. "I started the plague to challenge the damn vampires working for God. You see, my Father and I made a wager. Good versus evil, you know? Your family was merely collateral damage.

I took 'em. I can return 'em." A quick wave of his hand released the mob boss.

Gamino struggled to stand, weaved over to the chair by his fireplace, and slumped into it. "You can give them back to me?"

Lucifer smiled and polished his long, pointed nails on his three-piece black suit. "Well, of course. For a price, that is."

"What? Anything." The crime leader sank to his knees on his expensive tapestry rug.

"Well, I promised God not to mess with his beloved vampires, but I didn't swear not to screw with his pitiful humans. So, the cost is your soul, of course." Lucifer's smile widened on his face, and his blue eyes turned red.

Gamino nodded. "Is that all?"

"Well, you'll be working for me, of course. In Florence. You see, the place is a mess. Its inhabitants are confused and weak. I want to wreck them and their beloved city. You'll be my instrument of destruction."

Gamino stared into the face of the devil. "But why would you want to do that?"

The fallen angel threw back his head and laughed. The vibration from his voice shook the room. "Why, because I can. What else?"

"And, for this, you will return my family to me?" The gangster stood. His eyes narrowed. "No tricks? No bait and switch? You won't bring them back like those people in Stephen King's *Pet Sematary*? They'll be like they were before the plague?"

"Yes, yes… such details." Satan dismissed the thought with a wave of his hand. "You'll do it? Give me your soul to use as I wish?"

"Yes. If you restore my family… as they were before you took them… to me."

"Awh, there's the rub. You must first work to get them. Get it?"

"Yes. I get it," Gamino said as his den faded away, then vanished, and he found himself standing in the Palazzo Vecchio in Florence.

CHAPTER ONE

JAMES AND REIGN

James intrigues me.

Like my mother before me, I am fascinated by a vampire, and not just any vampire. My four paws pad along silently some twenty yards behind him. Spring has brought little green buds up through the dark earth. I take pleasure in almost floating over them so as not to crush them. I am wolf-born, so life in nature is precious to me.

James is not like the other vampires in our family. Kane, our leader, is intelligent but fierce. Zandra, his mate, is beautiful but deadly. Her ten brothers, the Morettis, are equally loyal to both but terrifying. James once had been Kane's servant. Zandra, at Kane's request, had turned him into the hybrid vampire Lycan he wished to be.

But now that his lifelong goal has been achieved, he wanders listlessly through the forest. After he fought with his master's family for God the Father and won over Satan, Kane's vampire family was granted everlasting peace.

This has not worked well for James. He is meant to serve. He longs for a new master, a real purpose.

As kindred, he lusts for the blood of battle. He tends to be more like the ten Moretti brothers. Peace and quiet bring them little pleasure. It's hard for me to imagine the meek, gray man Zeb Moretti swears James once was. As a hybrid, he is tall and somewhat handsome in his human visage but seemingly void of purpose.

James stops, turns toward me, and gives me a wistful smile. He sits on a fallen log and motions for me to join him. He speaks to me through telepathy. *Come, Reign. Sit beside me, miracle creature.*

I sniff the air, lick my chops, and wag my tail.

I approach and press my salt-and-pepper-colored fur against his knee. I press my nose against his arm hoping for his fingernails.

He scratches my head. *Kane is right. You shouldn't exist, but you do.*

My icy-blue eyes search his slate-gray ones. *Why do you say I shouldn't exist?*

His smile is wry, barely visible. *Because you are the product of the mating between Moon Blood, Kane's vampire-wolf progeny, and Enzo, her spirit wolf. Such a coupling has never occurred.*

I stand, alerting to the sound of quickly moving footsteps.

James springs up as well, and we both spy a human male running through the forest toward Kane's Tuscany wine estate.

James and I, with our vampire speed, are on him in an instant, blocking his progress further. James holds out his hands, palms facing the balding, older man.

Tears stream from the man's brown eyes, and the crazed look on his face raises the hairs on the back of my neck. Growling, I crouch and bare my teeth.

"Whoa!" James commands. "Where are you going?"

The human tries to get around James, who stands at least a head taller and blocks the man's passage again. The man grows more agitated. "The vampires, Brogio's son… must get to them." He draws a gun from his coat and points it at us. "Let me go!"

James laughs.

The man points the weapon at James's chest and fires.

I watch the bullet hit my friend's expansive chest, flatten against it, and then slowly fall to the ground.

The man wipes tears from his eyes, points the gun again, and fires into James's face. He has gone beyond reason.

This time, the bullet smashes into the hybrid vampire Lycan's face, sticks on his left cheek, and rolls off.

"What the hell!" The man takes a step back. "Are you one of them?"

"By 'one of them,' if you mean vampire, yes. I am James. Bullets, blades, even fire have no effect on me. Nothing can pierce me or my clothing."

Hope springs into the human's pathetic eyes. "Then, you can take me to Kane!"

James looks up into the sun and sighs. "No, unfortunately, not at this hour. Perhaps later. Or tell me why you are here. Kane no longer should be troubled by conflict."

The man waves the gun. "What do you mean? He's the one that caused our problems. He must resolve them." His voice rises to almost a feminine screech. "We need another potion."

Realization floods over James's face as I go into one of the trances I have inherited from my spirit-wolf father. This one is of the past. Citizens of the entire city of Florence are being attacked by humanlike zombies. Those not devoured turn. Kane makes a potion, and Alexander, one of his coven leaders, takes the elixir to a human. The same human who shot James in the face. He's the CEO of a large pharmaceutical company. The human mass-produces the potion. Vials are put in the water all over the world. Zombies return to their human state. But Kane adds something in the potion to make people forget. A mother stares down at an empty crib, her eyes vacant. A man examines a photo seemingly trying to recognize those around him in the picture. A teenager walks endlessly looking into the faces of strangers.

Everyone in Florence has forgotten their previous lives. Forgetting the people they lost prevents pain and grief—for a time.

When I recover from my trance, I connect my mind to James's and know he is already aware of these details.

The CEO takes out a white handkerchief and wipes his eyes and sweaty face.

The musty stench of fear, the acidic smell of confusion, and flowery scent of sorrow mingle, assaulting my nose. He is on the verge of insanity.

He rubs his free hand against his pants leg and begins to sob.

"Why do you need another potion?" James attempts to get the man to calm down by getting him to provide more details.

"Because none of us can remember! I have photographs of me and a woman and children, but I don't know who they are. Clothing and possessions are scattered throughout my house that belong to a woman and children, but I am the only person living in my home. I have no memory of them. I am only one of many. Everyone in Florence has been unable to sleep, work, or function. The city is in chaos. Everyone is going insane. Please, Kane has to help us." The man becomes even more agitated and begins to tear at his shirt. His eyes widen. "Take me to Kane! You might be impervious to bullets, but I'm betting the wolf isn't!" He swings the gun in my direction.

Just as he fires it, James twists the man's hand away from me, and the bullet explodes and enters my attacker's brain. The CEO's head explodes, and blood splatters everywhere— everywhere but on James's silver garments or body.

Catching the man before he falls to the ground, James bites into his own wrist as he lowers the CEO.

Blood, the color of silver, drips into the human's mouth.

James extends one long fingernail and reaches inside the hole in the man's head and fishes out the bullet.

Minutes pass. The hole in the man's head begins to close.

I lick my chops and sit on my haunches.

James smiles.

The CEO begins to stir. The hole in his head and the trauma the bullet has inflicted slowly knits together and vanishes. His eyes flutter.

James brings him to a sitting position. "Easy now. You are just recovering from a bullet to your brain. It may take a bit for you to come back to your senses, if that's possible."

The CEO looks from James to me. Apparently, the bullet has scrambled his brain, because the first words out of his mouth are "That wolf has the bluest eyes I've ever seen."

James laughs. "You should see his mother and grandfather."

The man blinks. "You are a vampire, you said?"

"Yes. A hybrid vampire Lycan."

"Then how can you be here in the daylight?" The man gingerly pats his head where the bullet had entered.

James ignores the question and helps the man to stand. "What is your name?"

"I am Paolo Gianetti…" The man scrunches his eyebrows as if he wants to add more to the sentence.

"Yes. We know."

The man staggers and falls against James.

I growl and move between them.

"Careful. I don't want Reign to accidentally bite you because he thinks you're trying to harm me." He steadies Gianetti.

"Why?"

"Hmm… let's just say I doubt I could bring you back from that one." James eyeballs me and shakes his head. "One bite from him, and you'd be dead in a heartbeat."

Looking at Gianetti, James points to another fallen tree trunk. "Now that you have calmed down, here's what we're going to do… Sit and fill me in on what's happening in Florence. Then, go home. I will talk to Kane and see how we can help you. I swear to you that I will seek you out and let you know if we can provide a solution. All right?"

James's calm demeanor and soothing voice have a deep effect on the man. He nods and sits. James joins him, and I position myself next to the hybrid vampire Lycan.

I don't know why I want to protect and follow James. I don't have a blood connection to him as my grandfather, Snow Blood, has to Brogio or my mother, Moon Blood, has to Kane. Perhaps fate draws us together, or something greater. Maybe, like my father Enzo, I am to be James's spirit wolf.

As Gianetti talks, I know James has found a purpose to embrace, at least for now.

CHAPTER TWO

KANE'S FAMILY

James and I see Gianetti safely to his Mercedes parked a mile away from where we first encountered him. As we watch him drive away back toward Florence, we both sense familiar presences lurking in the forest behind us.

You can stop hiding now, boys. James smirks as he turns and uses telepathy, our preferred method of communication.

Hiding? We didn't want to give the poor man a heart attack while he was still recovering from having his brains blown out. Zeb Moretti laughs and emerges from around a tall maple tree.

The oldest of Zandra Moretti's ten brothers, Zeb
dwarfs James, who grew to six-feet-three inches
when he was transformed into a hybrid vampire
Lycan. At least, that's what I have heard Zandra
tell Kane.

From deeper in the forest, the other nine
brothers join us. Each appears as tall as their older
brother. Their broad shoulders lead down to
strong, muscular arms. Each has long dark hair in
varying shades of brown or black. Their olive skin
and golden eyes match those of their sister.

If they were not my friends, I would be
spooked by them, even in their human forms. Once
they turn into whatever creature they wish to be in
battle, or on the hunt, they are terrifying.

All are loyal to their sister, but none more
than Zeb. Whenever he looks at her, his golden
eyes melt with love and devotion.

Zachary, the second oldest brother, seems to
grow larger as he playfully tosses the now meatless
leg bone of a moose over to rugged but charming

Zale, who grins and catches the large bone with one hand without looking at it. He flips it over his head to Zander, the shy one, who gnaws on it and throws it over to Zeno, who catches and tosses it to Zindel and Zane. They play catch with it, laughing as they do until Zane turns unexpectedly and clips Zeno in the head with the bone. *Catch this, you bonehead!*

Zeno immediately takes off after the other two back into the woods. They are always together in all their efforts, play or battle.

Zohar strolls over to James and gives him a nonchalant and carefree nod. He is the most laid-back of the brothers, and his inner spirit embraces freedom and fun.

Zoltan, the sensitive one and my mother's favorite, soon joins us. *Do you think Gianetti will be all right? He seemed unhinged back there.*

James nods. *He will be fine. I compelled him to calm down and wait for us to respond to him before he left.*

What are you blubbering about, Zoltan? You worry too much. Zylon scowls as he joins us and glances at his brother.

Zoltan shrugs and touches my head and gives me a good ear rub.

Zylon polishes off the other leg bone of the moose, tosses it on the ground, and licks his fingers. His face is covered with scars because, according to James, he always takes the most aggressive chances in battle. Of all the brothers, he is only second to Zeb in battle prowess.

Zeno, Zane, and Zindel join us, not wanting to miss anything James might share.

Even though James had been a servant in life, as kindred, he commands the respect of Zandra's brothers. They almost see him as an advocate for them with Kane.

Zeb searches James's face. *Does this problem in Florence bring us some adventure we can pursue?*

We're weary of the peace and quiet, Zachary interjects. *Kane may not want to mix it up with an enemy or two, but we do.* He slaps Zylon on the back. *We had the time of our lives when every god, goddess, devil, demon, zombie, berserker, and every known variety of creatures were out to destroy our master!*

Let's go find some problems and break a bunch of heads. Zylon draws up to his full, immense height. His voice comes out like a growl. *We were eavesdropping around you earlier. We know there's trouble in Florence.*

I must step back and crane my neck to see his face.

Then, you know as much as I do. Let's go talk it out with Kane and Zandra.

∞

Instead of utilizing our lightning-fast speed to return home, James chooses to stroll the two miles back to Kane's Chianti Hills wine estate. He appears to be searching in his mind for the right words to convince Kane to become involved with the problem in Florence, which is just a short distance away.

The sun is setting over the red-tile roof of the three-story nineteenth-century stone estate villa housing fifteen bedrooms.

The workers in the adjacent wine cellars are just reaching their cars and are ready to drive home to their families.

We wait in the forest that extends out from the estate with its teeming prey that allows us to quench our bloodlust. We all follow Brogio's golden rule of never harming humans or using them for sustenance on purpose. We keep our distance until the last car is gone before we head to the large red front door that the brothers must stoop under to enter.

I skip across the marbled black-and-white tile of the large entrance past the circular stairs next to the entry.

As I pad into the den, the ever-present fire is smoldering in the oversized rock fireplace—a tradition Kane carries on from Brogio, his sire and the original vampire. None of us can feel its warmth, but we enjoy the ambience it provides.

I love the feel of the rich maroon and blue handmade Italian rugs covering the wide mahogany plank floors under my paws. I remember my mother telling me how she had loved to roll on the priceless artifacts, but James, the servant, had always chased her off.

Dark-stained cypress furniture fills this room. Beautiful artwork by the great masters lines the walls. I pause in front of *Bacchus* by da Vinci. The god of wine is an appropriate portrait for this estate. The subject's half-naked human body looks like something that would compare to Zoltan's sleek, muscular one.

I shuffle into the dining room with its massive table that seats twenty people, go through the kitchen door, and sniff the aroma of fresh blood being prepared in the black-and-white kitchen with stainless-steel appliances.

I wander into Kane's large library and study, just off the den. It connects to a laboratory filled with experiments at different stages. I sneeze when the acrid smell of the lab hits my nose.

Waiting for Kane and Zandra to rise, I saunter into the recreation room with a wall-sized television, a complete entertainment center, pool table, and another bar. It opens through French doors to an elegant pool in the back of the house. A cabana outfitted with a table to seat twelve for serving meals sits poolside.

Ripples dance within the water tempting me to take a swim, but the fading sunlight alerts me that Kane and Zandra will soon awaken. I return to the den and join James and the brothers.

I hear a snick of a door closing, and hand in hand, Kane and Zandra stroll down the stairs from the "sleep room" with no windows and its king-sized, four-poster bed, where the first blood son of

Brogio sleeps safely with Zandra and my mother, Moon Blood, during the daylight hours. Enzo, my father, and Noble, who replaced James as servant, persist in watching over them as they rest, even though three years have passed since a threatening incident. James now occasionally joins them, as do I, but those times have become less frequent as the silver-haired ex-servant has become more restless.

No one would suspect that these two beautiful beings are deadly vampires who have chosen to live in peace with the world. Both dark haired, Zandra is only a few inches shorter than the tall, broad-shouldered being beside her. Kane is known for his intelligence and great knowledge. Like her husband, Zandra is the first blood child of an original. He is the progeny of the first vampire. She is the daughter of the original werewolf. Kane made her and her brothers hybrid vampire Lycans. Though ancient, like all kindred, they are youthful in appearance. James and I have not existed long. I was born two years ago. James was turned only three years ago.

Kane and Zandra are surprised to see all of us gathered in the den. The master of the house offers a warm greeting. *How wonderful to see everyone.*

Zandra kneels next to me and wraps her arms around my neck. *Reign, my miracle boy, how handsome you are. I know it's only been a day, but every time I see you, I just want to squeeze you, turn into a wolf, and run beside you.*

She smells of forest and rain on a spring afternoon.

I hang my neck over her shoulder and press into her.

She obliges with a thorough scratching with her long nails. I snort and back away when it begins to feel too good. I fear my legs might give way.

Zandra laughs and joins her husband as he pours her a glass of his vintage wine at the long wall-to-wall bar to the right of the fireplace.

Enzo and Moon Blood, my parents, jump down the stairs. They are a picture of opposites. He is dark black with golden eyes. Her long fur is solid white. Her blue eyes peer into mine as she trots up to me. She gives my face a thorough washing with her rough tongue.

I am the combination of the two of them with black, white, and gray fur but with her bluest of eyes.

You have had some small adventure today. She steps back and sits in front of me. My father joins her.

Yes. Kane turns his furrowed brow toward me. *No need to fill us in. We see what you do; you know that.*

Zandra twirls her glass of wine, gulps it down, and turns to take the tall crystal glass of AB Neg that Noble offers to her and Kane. *You know,*

James, that my husband no longer wishes to get involved with the trials of humans. God the Father promised this family everlasting peace after we fought Satan for him.

James runs his hands through his long silver hair and crosses his arms. No longer the meek servant, he juts out his chin and grits his teeth. *Master.* He looks deeply into Zandra's eyes. *The confusion and turmoil are partly because of the memory-erasing potion used to cure the zombies. But there's more.*

Kane drains his glass of blood and sets it down. *Yes, I know, James. Gamino and his mob have taken control of Florence and gotten rid of the mayor and the legislative body they call the Consiglio Comunale or City Council. The thirty-six councilors elected every five years contextually to the mayoral elections have been murdered and replaced. So have the executive body, or giunta communale, of seven assessors presided over by a directly elected mayor.*

James steps forward. *Yes. The head of this country's Mafia is in charge. Gamino's second-in-command, Luce Fairento, leads a group of henchmen who are killing off people in the streets and wreaking havoc. They're stealing from homes and businesses, raping women, and raining terror on these passive people who are slowly losing their minds.*

Kane picks up a second glass of wine. *I'm willing to bet that they are both under Satan's control.*

What! Zandra whirls around, her golden eyes wide with fury. *We defeated the bastard. He can't interfere anymore.*

Ah. Kane smiles as he holds up one finger. *There's the rub. He promised not to interfere with vampires... He promised nothing about humans.*

Zeb, Zachary, and Zylon rush forward, eyes filled with excitement. They all speak at once. *Then, we can do something... fight them off... help the humans!*

Massacre the devil worshippers! Zylon growls out, his body quivering with anticipation.

James holds out his hands, palms facing the three brothers. *No. First, we must deal with the human turmoil left after the zombie infection killed so many.* He turns to Kane. *They are slowly going mad, haunted by things they can't explain because the potion used to cure the plague erased the survivors' memories of those they lost.* His questioning eyes morph from deep gray to silver.

Kane folds his arms and spreads his legs clad in black jeans. *You are going to ask me to make another potion.*

James lifts his head and juts out his chin. *Why not? Gianetti, the CEO you used before, will mass-produce it for Florence. Regaining their memories will help them to cease their ever-growing madness.*

I sit back on my haunches and wonder what Kane might have been thinking when he dared to erase all those memories.

Kane crooks his neck at me. His eyes narrow and turn momentarily red. *That would mean we get involved in their business. I cannot. I don't want to risk getting involved. It might give Satan a reason to start meddling with us again.*

My mother walks to his side and licks his hand.

He smiles. His love for her calms his wrath at my daring to question him. He stares at her for a moment. They appear to enjoy a silent conversation blocked from the rest of us.

I know of a better way. One that doesn't involve another potion.

Zandra takes her husband's arm. She frowns as she reads his mind. *You are thinking of Adam.*

Adam? James moves closer to his master and her mate. Realizing he has not paid them the proper respect they are due, he lowers his eyes and looks at the floor. *Do you mean Brogio and Selene's son?*

Yes. Zandra smiles, reaches out, and lifts James's chin. *No need to behave as the servant, James. You have earned the right to speak your mind.*

James looks into her golden eyes and then over into Kane's dark-brown orbs. *But what can a five-year-old boy do to solve this problem?*

Placing a hand on James shoulder, Kane points him to the large stuffed chairs in front of the fireplace. *Sit with us.*

Kane pulls Zandra into the chair with him, and James plops into the one opposite them. I sit next to him, and Mother and Father settle into their maroon satin and suede beds next to the fireplace. The brothers, who have maintained their human form, all sprawl out on the floor, taking up all the extra space in the den.

Kane eyes me for a moment and takes a glass of wine from the tray Noble is passing around. *Like Reign, Adam is a miracle. Like Moon Blood and Enzo's progeny, Adam has magic.*

Adam was born of two vampires turned human. Historically, as you know, vampires have magical qualities. Because Brogio was the first, the magic in him as a vampire was powerful. Couple with that the fact that both Brogio and Selene were touched by God through the angels.

James slides forward in his chair and clasps his hands. *So, you're saying that Adam has super magical powers?*

I'm saying—Kane takes a sip of his wine—*that Adam is destined to be the most powerful wizard who has ever lived.*

The brothers all sit bolt upright at Kane's words.

Wizard! Zachary cries out.

Most powerful? The other nine brothers say in unison.

Kane nods, and Zandra stands.

She crosses her arms and shakes her head. *There's only one problem.*

What? James stands to face her.

How can you even think to bring a child into this?

Kane stands and wraps an arm around his wife.

Zandra whirls in his arms. *I can't believe you condone bringing this child under the potential scrutiny of Satan!*

Kane shakes his head. *Do you honestly think Lucifer Morningstar isn't aware of Adam and what he will be able to do in the future?*

Zandra stamps her foot so hard on Kane's that his smile turns to a grimace. *Why does that matter? Putting him out there… to do what? Can he make a potion? Use his undeveloped magic to fight the devil?*

Kane pulls his wife closer to him. *Just as newly made vampires discover their gifts, Adam is already realizing his abilities. Do not think of him as helpless or undeveloped.* He looks at James and then me.

I stand and press against James's legs. *How can I serve James?*

Kane smiles wistfully. *It's up to you and James to convince first Brogio and Selene, and then Adam, to use his magic to restore the memories of the people of Florence.*

A thrill runs through my body, and I realize what I'm feeling is coming from James.

My mother Moon Blood's voice fills my brain. *This is why you were created, Reign. You are linked to James now, just as surely as I am to Kane.*

Enzo's deep voice joins hers. *I know not why, but a higher purpose awaits you, son.*

Their thoughts are crowded as the Moretti brothers' voices cry out, *We will go with them! We will help.*

James turns to his kindred. *Come with us. But perhaps try not to overwhelm our request by letting me do the talking. Yes?*

Laughter explodes as the brothers take turns slapping James on the back and head to the bar to celebrate their impending adventure.

CHAPTER THREE

ADAM

"Put upon" are the words I'd use to describe flying in a kennel in the belly of a private jet to Nova Scotia.

The sight of a large wolf will terrify Kane's crew, James explains.

Really? I snort. *You mean, more so than those lumbering hybrid vampire-werewolf brothers? You'd think the crew would be used to seeing strange creatures flying with Kane.*

The crew changes out often. At least, you don't have to fly in a coffin like your mother had to, James retorts as he shuts the cargo-hold door.

My only comforting thoughts are that the Z brothers are way too large to fit into even the spacious seating accommodations on Kane's airplane. Misery loves company. At least, I cando something about my situation. Using my magic, I close my eyes and focus on being on the outside of the crate. Before I know it, I'm out! *Easy-peasy. My father Enzo says to use magic whenever I feel it necessary. This time is a must.* Settling down on the jet floor, I am lulled to sleep by the roar of the engines.

I think about teleporting back into the crate as we land but decide not to waste my energy. I am surprised when James, instead of a baggage handler, opens the cargo-hold door.

Just as I suspected. He shakes his head. *Please climb into the crate before you terrify everyone at the VIP terminal.* He opens the kennel door and motions with his head for me to enter. *So, we can add teleportation to your list of talents.*

Yes, and if I'd thought of it earlier, I would have transported us both here instead of flying.

You can do that? James peers inside the crate at me.

I snort and stare back at him. *Looks like it.*

He hoists the kennel, with me in it, out of the cargo hold like it's weightless, puts me on the waiting cart, throws his overnight bag on it, and joins the brothers who are already starting to draw a crowd.

One woman approaches Zeb and asks him if she can take a selfie with him. "You must be related to Jason Momoa! You look just like him, only bigger."

She finally ends up having one of the people inside the terminal take a photo with all ten brothers.

As she hustles off, James growls, *Stop drawing attention to yourselves.*

What? Zeb rears back his head. *We didn't do anything.*

They all break into laughter as we enter the terminal, and everyone stops and stares at the eleven large men accompanying a huge kennel through their midst. I make myself as small as possible not to be noticed. But I needn't have worried. All eyes are on silver-haired James in his white pants and shirt and silver belt and the hulking Z brothers, who I must admit are fine specimens. The other travelers must think James is a movie star with his bodyguards.

Three limos await us since only four brothers can fit in one big car.

Finally, I'm set free and bounce into the first limo. The driver is obviously used to the unexpected as James and two other brothers crowd in. He doesn't bat an eye.

The drive from Halifax Stanfield takes slightly less than an hour, and we all partake of the plentiful bags of human blood stored in the limo refrigerator.

I see Brogio still has choice blood flown in from Mexico for his kindred visitors. James pours part of a bag into a crystal bar glass as Zeb and Zachary bite off a piece of the heavy plastic containers and guzzle them down.

Yes, Zeb mumbles between gulps, *and I'm glad Kane carries on that tradition. I enjoy not always having to hunt for prey.*

James finds a crystal bowl and pours a bag of O Neg into it for me to savor. I take after my mother and grandfather and have always preferred it to other blood types. It has the sweet smell of cinnamon and has a slight bite that lingers in my mouth and always makes my mouth water.

As I finish my nectar and take a moment to let it send a fiery comfort to my veins, I notice the car entering Brogio's Wolfville, Nova Scotia wine estate. The large entrance gate, flanked by two large, beautiful metal dragons, swings open in welcome. The long drive to the house is lined with beautiful tall oaks. The first thing I notice about the multilevel house is its unusually tall front door as the former vampires throw it open and welcome us with open arms.

I have only met Brogio and Selene a few times and am always taken aback by their physical presence. Both seem to be in their mid-twenties. Brogio's long silver hair falls past his broad shoulders. He's very tall—almost a head taller than Kane and more so than James. I see why the entryway is so tall. His eyes are violet, and his navy shirt and jeans combined with his silver hair make them look dark purple. Selene always surprises me. She is the light version of Zandra. She is tall like the hybrid vampire Lycan, and her silver hair almost touches her waist. Her eyes are as brilliantly blue as mine. I think she is the most beautiful human female I have ever seen.

James and the brothers lumber out to hug each of them, and I hang back in the limo to observe. I try to imagine how the two of them were once vampires and, by the grace of God, are no longer.

A little boy, almost a miniature replica of his father with shaggy silver hair and purple eyes, rushes out along with my grandparents, Snow Blood and Nova. He leaps into James's arms and then wiggles free to jump into each of the brothers' awaiting arms. He squeals with delight as they spread out and toss him among them. He flies in the air from Zeb to Zachary, Zohar to Zane, Zindel to Zeno, Zale to Zander, and Zoltan to Zylon, who takes off running with the boy, throwing him in the air and catching him. The normally gruff hybrid is filled with laughter that rumbles from his chest.

I sit in amazement until Snow Blood and Nova hop into the car and lick me from head to paw, turning me over and rolling me around, until I jump out of the limo and lead them in a merry chase around the area between the estate house and the winery, each layered with wooden beams and levels. I notice as I romp past that the winery contains large wraparound windows so that those inside can see the outdoor beauty of Nova Scotia and the distant mountains.

Suddenly, I feel a weight upon my back and a child's loud giggle and realize Adam has teleported himself onto me, like I'm a horse to be ridden. He takes hold of the long hairs on my neck, and I take off jumping, bucking, and dashing here and there. His laughter magnifies until I slide to a stop and sit back on my haunches. He scoots off, skips around to my face, and takes my face in his small hands. "You are Reign, and we're going to be great friends. You are my dogs' grandson." He smiles and whispers in my ear, "And you are filled with magic, like me."

I stare into his very intelligent purple eyes. A shock of platinum forelock hangs over one eye. He wraps his small arms around me and sighs. "We will make mischief together, yes?"

I snort, and my parents and their now-humans join us.

Brogio picks up his son, tosses him in the air, and laughs. "Come, let's take our friends in for a visit."

Adam's violet eyes never leave me as I follow everyone into the house.

∞

The hour is late. I am grateful all of us are daywalkers and can sleep at night.

After our hosts offer us a hefty assortment of human blood, and their chef cooks up a smorgasbord of meat for the brothers, Adam entertains us with amazing magical pranks.

"Let's play hide-and-seek!" The boy's laughter explodes through the room as he vanishes in front of my eyes.

James, the brothers, and I spread out and find him in a kitchen cabinet. As James reaches for him after pulling open his hideout's door, the boy disappears.

"Let's try upstairs." Zylon half-laughs with a growl.

We all vault up to the second floor and find him hiding under the bed in his parents' former safe room.

Zylon tries to grab him and is immediately teleported into the Jacuzzi next to the pool.

I sense to where the brother has vanished and rush down to bark and run around the pool, while all others stand around bent over in laughter.

Apparently, Zylon is not amused and smells like a wet dog for hours after.

Finally getting Adam to bed, Brogio and Selene join James and the brothers for a glass of vintage port. I lie next to my grandmother Nova as she sleeps on her fancy bed. Grandfather lies at his master's feet.

I look around and notice missing relatives. I concentrate and scan Brogio's mind for my answer and discover my mother's siblings and their families now reside in the forest as wolves should.

Brogio twirls his crystal glass and looks over at James. "When Kane called and said you wanted to visit, he indicated you need a favor." His violet eyes look from James to each of the ten brothers sitting in chairs that black-clad servants have brought in for them. "I imagine it's a large favor if it takes eleven hybrids and a vampire spirit-wolf to ask it."

James takes a long draw from his glass, holds it in his mouth, and swallows. "First, let me tell you why we need the favor."

I close my eyes and listen as James retells all that has come to pass.

"So, it appears"—Brogio stands—"that Kane's potion combined with the Mafia has made a mess of Florence."

James nods his agreement.

"And Kane thinks we can help you as opposed to making another potion?"

James sighs. "Not you. Adam."

Selene lunges to her feet. "No!"

James stands. "Hear me out, please, both of you."

Brogio turns toward Selene and wraps his arms around his wife. "We will not entertain any proposal that puts our son in harm's way, James."

"No. I don't suggest that in the least." James sets down his glass, stands, and grips the back of his chair.

"Then what are you suggesting?" Brogio's violet eyes grow wider.

Selene stands in her husband's arms and vigorously shakes her head to the negative.

"Adam is full of magic. We had hoped Adam could draw upon his magic from afar, when needed. We don't suggest he go into the fray with us. Just cast his magic to unlock the memories of the people of Florence."

Selene takes in a deep breath, hugs her husband, and returns to her chair. "Oh, is *that* all? A tall order for a little boy."

"He wouldn't have to leave this estate," Zeb interjects and gets a sharp glare from James.

Brogio begins to pace in front of the fireplace. "So, let me get this straight. You're asking that Adam use his magic to unlock the minds of a city full of people?" He turns to Selene. "Can he even do that?"

His wife rubs her forehead with a hand and bites her lower lip. Her eyebrows rise and lower.

I sense turmoil within her.

"What—" Brogio stares at her. Slow realization spreads across his face. "What did you see him do that you didn't share with me?"

Selene slowly raises his eyes to her husband. "I took him into town the other day. He turned all the townspeople into puppies. When I convinced him to turn them back, he did so, and they didn't appear to even know anything had happened to them."

"Good God, woman! Why would you keep that from me?"

She shrugs. "I knew you'd be upset. He likes to use his magic to have fun. He's just a little boy." She turns to James. "But he's wiser than he appears. He's an old soul born of two ancients. I think he knows he has great power, but I don't think he's ready to face the fact that he is a force with which to be reckoned. He just wants to be a child."

James walks around his chair, sits, and leans toward her. "Think of how much he would be helping so many suffering people. Do we have your permission to talk to Adam about this?"

Brogio closes his eyes, deep in thought.

I can sense the struggle within him.

He finally opens his eyes and looks at his wife who gently nods yes. Brogio sits on the arm of his wife's stuffed chair and rubs her shoulder. "The problem is convincing Adam. Do you think you can do that?"

"No." James's jewel-like eyes sparkle as he looks over at me. "But Reign can."

∞

I lap up the bowl of O Neg that Selene has so generously poured for me in the pristine kitchen. I lick the bowl clean and nibble up the small smatterings of the nectar that have splattered on the black-and-white marble floor.

Adam giggles as he watches me flop over and roll on my back as ecstasy rushes through my body.

He eats a bowl of Grape-Nuts and crunches them with his teeth as he laughs at the sound he makes.

I sit up and wait for him to finish.

He jumps down from the high stool at the breakfast bar and squats next to me so that our eyes meet.

You already know what I want to ask of you, don't you?

The boy's face grows solemn. *I will be asked many questions like yours throughout my adult life. I am not ready to deal with them yet.*

I place one of my large paws on his lap, and he sits back on his heels so that I look down into his eyes. *Like me, you were born with responsibility. We have a greater purpose than most. People's lives and happiness will often depend upon us. You can have both your childhood and serve the greater good.*

Adam wiggles closer to me and crosses his knees. *How?*

You will stay here. We will only call on you from afar when we need your magic. The rest of the time, you can play the role of a child. We will only call upon you when the need is great.

The boy stands. I join him, and Selene watches us closely as we walk out of the kitchen and into the den. She follows and joins Brogio who is reading the newspaper. James and the brothers are scattered around the large room just waiting.

Adam sits on one of the many beautiful tapestry rugs and points for me to sit next to him. *And you think I can retrieve the memories of almost four-hundred-thousand people?*

You turned forty-two hundred people into puppies and then restored them, and they had no memory of it happening. What do you think? I stare into his eyes. *Think of it as a challenge, or a game.*

The child gives me a look that triggers the vision of a very old wizard.

You will live a very long time, Adam, and you will be the most powerful wizard who ever existed. Is there really anything beyond your ability to control? Don't you want to see if you have limitations now?

Adam smiles. *You challenge me, spirit wolf. I like that. Yes. When you call upon me, I will test my strength.*

Why can we not test it now while we are all here together?

The child springs to his feet. *You want me to do it now? With no time to prepare?*

How much time do you need to prepare?

To cast a spell to alter the target's memories of an event that took place any time in the person's past requires a certain level of understanding, let alone hundreds of thousands of people. A memory modifier can't affect how the person behaves, especially if the memory... blocks... no... contra... what's the word?

Contradicts?

Yes, that's it. If the memory contradicts the person's natural inclinations or beliefs. I need to think on it. It's the reverse of Obliviate.

What's that? I stand and stare at his face.

It's the spell for erasing a memory.

You have a big vocabulary for a little boy.

Adam looks at Brogio. *I come from one who is as ancient as time. He is human now, but he passed all his knowledge to me. The same goes for my mother. Why is it a surprise that I have such intellect?*

I walk around him, and he giggles. *I like it when you focus on me. So, I'll do it, but you must play with me first.*

For how long? I glance at James who sits waiting patiently. I know he can hear everything that transpires between the boy and me.

Until I'm satisfied! Adam moves quickly and mounts my back. *Let's go.* With a wave of his hand, the front door swings wide, and I take it as my cue.

As I run past James, he stands. "It's settled. Adam has agreed to help us, after Reign entertains all his wishes."

The boy whispers in my ear. "Use your vampire speed. I want to know how it feels to be lightning!"

I have a feeling that Kane will meet his match in the thirst for knowledge even before Adam grows up.

∞

Adam puts me through my paces. That day, I sprint from the estate to Wolfville and then all the way to Halifax. The boy holds on and screams and yells in delight the entire time.

We play hide-and-seek the entire next day in the forest using our powers of invisibility. I grow weary of appearing and disappearing, but Adam pushes it from sunrise to sunset.

The following day, he has me transform into multiple beings from a woman to a cat to a horse. You name it. He has me become it. He imitates me by transforming into me, his mother and father, and even James. I'm astounded. I feel as if he is absorbing my ability to transform.

Later, he rides on my back and instructs me to take down small pray so he can understand what it's like to hunt and sustain myself. Selene is not happy about that one. Brogio shrugs and comments, "We did it."

I am gorged by the end of that play period.

The next day, as we walk in the woods together, he turns to me. His purple eyes search my face. *Why is your bite so deadly?*

I inherited it from my grandfather and mother.

But how did Snow get it?

We walk a bit further where a lake nestles in the distance. I stop and sit back on my haunches. *Kane told us that the goddess Artemis gave it to Snow as a gift of protection. She coveted my grandfather and wanted him to belong to her, but as you know, he is forever loyal to your father...* Out of the corner of my eye I notice a strange, large ripple in the lake water. I sense danger and instantly push Adam behind some nearby bushes.

The boy cries out, "What are you—"

His words are drowned out by the roar of a beast unequaled by any other. It rises from the lake about fifty yards away from us. The monster furiously shakes the water droplets from its body.

Adam's eyes search mine. *That thing must be a lake monster.* Closing his eyes, the boy appears to search his memory. *My father and Kane fought a similar creature many years ago.*

The creature emerges from the lake. The creature is monstrous in size and shape, and its almond-shaped eyes survey its surroundings. Ugly beyond belief, with a downturned mouth and cleft head, it looks like a combination of a cat with deformed human characteristics. Large growths cover its enormous chest and back. I wonder if they function like body armor.

I growl and start to move forward, but Adam grabs me by the neck. *You can't fight this thing alone.* Adam's voice in my head is filled with concern. *It's a were-jaguar, a lycanthrope. Its bite is just as lethal as yours. It could kill you.*

How do you know? I swirl around to face him.

I told you. I have my father's memories. When this creature attacked them, Kane told

Brogio that he'd encountered them once in Romania. One of his coven members died in agony from its bite.

I ignore the creature's roars and sit down.

And it can move between worlds. That's what Kane said he learned in Romania. Plus, the thing is supernatural.

I stare fascinated with the creature who must be head and shoulders taller than Brogio's seven feet. It looks more like a tanker truck than anything. *How do we fight that?* Then realization floods through my brain. *Could Satan have gotten wind of our combining forces and sent this thing after us?* Shock ripples through my body at how it has surprised us.

A noise in the distance alerts the monster, and it turns and runs along the lake away from us with a speed that matches mine. A fallen tree lies in the middle of its path. The creature stoops, lifts the massive trunk with its deformed human hands, and throws the broken tree with a deafening scream through the woods, almost as a warning to anything lurking about.

Adam almost cackles under his breath. *I bet that thing can bench-press a car with one hand!* Realization sparkles through the child's eyes, and he grabs my shoulder. *Silver will kill it, Reign. That's how Brogio and Kane killed it before. It's the only metal that can pierce its body. And silver heals at human speed.*

I snort. *Great. Where do we get it?*

Adam smiles, closes his eyes, and conjures up a bow and a dozen silver arrows.

I snort again and note the monster is about twenty-five yards from us. *We need to get closer to it.*

Keep in mind—Adam pulls a silver arrow from its quiver—*that thing can hear a person's pulse just by standing nearby. It will detect us if we get much closer.*

I think for a second. *I will distract him. You run behind him as he chases me and unload those arrows into his backside.*

Adam grips my neck with his tiny free hand. *But it's as fast as you.*

No matter. I shake his hand loose. *I won't let it take you down. You're more important to this world. If it gets me, you dematerialize and run home for help.*

We could do that now, the boy counters.

But it could track us down. At least, if you go home while it's busy demolishing me, James and the brothers can fight with you.

I sprint forward and ignore the boy's screams in my brain.

The creature's keen hearing alerts, and it spins and roars, sending a shiver up my spine.

The monster's footsteps shake the ground as it speeds after me. A sickly smell of rotted meat and burnt fur assault my nostrils.

I whiz forward. I can almost feel its hot breath on my rear. I swerve, and a magical Adam appears nearby and tries to plant a silver arrow in the creature's shoulder. Before the arrow can hit its mark, the creature vanishes. I almost crash into it as it rematerializes in front of me. I skid to a stop, flash to the right, and dematerialize.

This time, Adam hits the beast's shoulder with a silver arrow as I reappear some fifty feet away.

The beast screams like a large cat and dashes harder after me.

Adam disappears, and rushing through the trees as fast as I can, I wish I had that luxury but need to keep it focused on me.

I look back and see the creature almost on me as Adam appears and, with unimaginable speed, plants two arrows, one after the other, into the beast's head.

Momentarily stunned, the enraged beast plunges forward. Its screams shake the trees.

I skid to a stop, leap high in the air, sail over its downed body, race to it before it can move, and tear out its jugular.

It rolls over, its beady eyes roll back in its head, and it foams at the mouth, convulses, and dies.

Adam rushes up to me and empties the remaining silver arrows into its body.

I nudge his hand with my nose. *It's okay. The thing was dead.*

The monster mysteriously explodes into flames, reaffirming my suspicion that Satan could be behind it.

Adam throws down the bow. *That's okay. If Satan did send it, I wanted to make sure it wouldn't reanimate.* He turns to me and rubs my head. *We make a good team. We couldn't have done this without each other. But may I suggest something?*

What? I look into his eyes.

Let's not tell Mom and Dad about this if you want my help. This would put the brakes on them letting me help you.

I stare into his deep, dark eyes. *James and the brothers will know.*

Adam smiles. *They won't tell if you won't.*

∞

On the fifth day, the brothers grow restless and decide to hunt for larger prey. Adam insists I take him with them.

Selene refuses this. "Enough, already, Adam! It's time for you to hold up your end of this bargain. Let Reign rest and go prepare for this spell you must do."

The boy hangs his head and pads off to the laboratory that Brogio created for his first blood son Kane years ago. Looking back at his mother, he mumbles, "You're no fun."

James instantly pulls out his cell phone and dials Kane. "It's James. Can you have Noble make a visit to Paolo Gianetti to see if he's gotten his memory back? Adam will be casting the spell sometime soon." He waits, listening intently to the voice on the other end of the phone. "You'll go? That's great, but I know you don't want to get involved. No. Yes, I understand. Thank you."

He turns to Brogio and Selene. "Kane has to make a trip into Florence anyway, so he'll go and can give us immediate feedback through our mental connection."

I know there is no need for that as I crawl over to one of the luxurious beds that Brogio has had made for me. I fall immediately into a trance. I dream of Adam in the laboratory. He reads and masters the ninth level of a memory modifier spell. He repeats the words "Obliviate Novis" hundreds of thousands of times until, in my trance, I think my head will explode. Then, he transforms into a youthful, handsome man. I know this is Adam at age twenty-five. He wears his shaggy platinum hair just below his ears. He is very tall. Dressed in jeans and an Under Armour black T-shirt that stretches over broad shoulders, he is very much the carbon copy of his father. He transports himself to Florence and stands before Paolo Gianetti in the man's home. He says the words he has repeated over and over in my trance.

The pharma CEO falls to his knees sobbing and holding his head. He cries out, "I remember! I remember them. The ungodly attack upon our city. My wife, my children… oh, my God in Heaven. Why did I want to remember?"

I watch in disbelief in my dream as Adam splits into hundreds of thousands of copies of himself and visits every person in the city repeating "Obliviate Novis."

Exhausted from the vision, my world goes dark until I feel James's hand on my shoulder and see him crouching over me.

"Wake up, boy. Adam did it. You did it. The entire city of Florence is in mourning over the loss of their loved ones, even as they are being robbed and murdered by the Mafie. The heartbreak of what those citizens are experiencing renders them still defenseless against Gamino and his henchmen." James stands and turns to Zeb and his brothers. "It's time for us to return to Italy and deal with it."

Zeb and Zachary nod knowingly. Zane, Zindel, and Zeno slap each other on the backs. The others surround Zylon and morph in their excitement to giant werewolves. Bones crack and pop, fangs drop, furry pointed ears emerge from normal ones. They fall to all fours, and their backs elongate and shake. Hands begin to form into claws.

"Enough!" Zeb yells. "You'll rip up your clothes. Save it for the gangsters in Florence."

Zylon growls, "Save the fancy clothes for James!"

Adam emerges from the laboratory in his five-year-old form and claps his hands with glee at the sight of the emerging creatures.

Selene scoops him up and hugs him tight. "Yes, enough magic and transformations. Go with speed, and please don't call on our son too often."

Brogio joins her and shakes his head. "I'm afraid it's too late for that, my love. Our son has opened his Pandora's box."

INTERLOGUE

Lucifer Morningstar stands on the third floor next to Vito Gamino at the large floor-to-ceiling window of Florence's city hall, Palazzo Vecchio in Piazza della Signoria.

In his handsome human guise, Satan grits his teeth. "Damn those meddling vampires! Father has once again blocked me from their activities, but I know this is their doing."

Below them in the plaza, instead of going about their daily activities, people walk about despondent, listless. Some sit on benches quietly crying or staring straight ahead as if they can't believe what has happened. Shock is the prevalent mood in Florence this day.

Gamino reaches over and closes one of the smaller side windows. "I understand their pain. I've felt it for three years now."

Luce Fairento, Gamino's second-in-command Mafia henchman, stands in the plaza below on the ground and glances upward at them.

Lucifer gives the henchman a slight nod of his head. "Let's end these pathetic creatures' misery and give my ears a rest."

To Gamino's surprise, Fairento waves his arm, and a mob of his own men rush to join him in the plaza. Pulling out submachine guns, they mow down several hundred people below.

Surprise written over his face, Gamino turns to Satan. "What the hell? I didn't give that order."

"No." Lucifer smirks. "I did."

"Why? I've done everything you've asked of me. All my lieutenants are in power seats in the city government. I overthrew the mayor and have taken control. What more do you want? Why kill people you want to rule over?"

Lucifer laughs, pours a glass of Gamino's fine Scotch whisky, and gulps it down. "You're a fine corrupt politician, Vito. I like that. But you're too soft. You think you must rule the city in order to help the people. I don't care about the people. I just want their souls."

Gamino spins around in anger and stares at Satan. "What am I then? A figurehead?"

"Yes, you're a fine example of a corrupt leader in a dirty swamp of a government. Just like I want. You're my puppet." He points toward Fairento. "But he's my backup plan if you fail me."

Gamino's mouth drops. "He's reporting directly to you?"

"Well, why do you think he's gone about killing off people in the streets and wreaking havoc? I've had him steal from homes and businesses, rape women and boys, and generally rain terror on these passive people, who, up till now, were losing their minds. And this is what Fairento loves."

"You've undermined me all along." Gamino wipes sweat from his brow. "And my own men are deceiving me. To what end? Why?"

"Because I enjoy it, Vito. Fairento has given over to me like you never will. You only serve me to regain your family. Luce Fairento serves me because he is evil to the core. Like me, he enjoys pain and suffering."

"Then, why do you need me?" Gamino clenches his fists, and the veins stick out in his neck as he tries to hold back his anger.

"Because you still control the Italian mob faction. Once I infiltrate and indoctrinate all that you control, I will no longer need you."

"And then, you will restore my family as you promised?" Gamino touches the sleeve of Lucifer Morningstar's black jacket.

The devil's eyes turn from blue to red and stare at the hand that dares to touch his sleeve. "You bore me with details, Vito. Don't you have a council meeting to attend? I want that gun disarmament bill passed today. We can't have our little citizens able to defend themselves, can we?"

CHAPTER FOUR

THE BATTLE

Instead of taking the private jet back home with the brothers, I show James my ability to teleport from one location to the next. As the jet taxies down the runway, I look up at the hybrid vampire Lycan I consider my partner. *Take hold of the fur on my neck.*

As James grasps hold of me, the airport dissolves. Moments later, we are standing in the Palazzo Vecchio near the Piazza della Signoria.

Damn, Reign. You are talented. James runs his hand across his face as he lets go of my neck fur.

Our adjustment to our change of venue is cut short by gunfire. People fall like flies in the plaza.

What? I start to move forward, but James grabs my tail and pulls me back.

Wait, Reign. It looks like Gamino and his men are becoming more aggressive in their takeover. Let's get back to Kane's estate and regroup with Zandra's brothers. We don't want to attack without being prepared.

At James's words, I freeze. The scene in front of me goes to a tunnellike perspective. A sparkling-like headache assaults my brain. What I see are not normal gangsters. As my vision clears, James's steel-gray eyes search my face.

Where did you go? What did you see?

I saw a faction of these mobsters who are devil worshippers practicing black-magic arts. One of the men we just saw gunning down innocents is devoted to Satan and the real enforcer of his evil. It also looks like the people of the city have been put under a curfew, supposedly for their own protection. But there's something nefarious about it. We're up against more than we realize.

James crosses his arms and surveys the bloody landscape. *Can you tell how many?*

I can't give specific, but several hundred here in the city. I sit back on my haunches and look up at him.

As Kane suspected, Satan is behind the corruption here. Most likely the curfew allows the ruling faction to know where all the citizens are at night and keep more control over them. Forget going back to the estate. Can you take us to the airport so that we can enlist the Moretti brothers as soon as they land?

I would have laughed if I had been a person. *Ask me something difficult next time.*

∞

Zylon Moretti, morphed out to the max, does a triple somersault and lands on two giant hind paws in the middle of a poker table surrounded by ten devil-worshipping mobsters. All seven feet of him stands, hands on furry hips, surveying the alarmed men.

Each one of them looks more sinister than the next, but as Zylon's long fangs hang below his pointed chin and leak of saliva, they cower a bit. Several draw hand pistols and take aim at him.

The hybrid vampire Lycan's large ears wiggle in an almost humorous fashion.

Before any one of the mobsters can fire, Zylon swipes off the heads of five of his prey with one large sharp-clawed paw, then turns and beheads the other five before they can take a breath. Several pre-death fingers manage to squeeze off a shot but miss my sinister companion and hit, instead, the already dead bodies of their fellow partners in crime.

I can almost detect a grin on Zylon's ferocious face as he stares at the headless bodies slumped in their chairs.

Another vision just before our arrival revealed that Fairento, Gamino's right-hand henchman, had frightened off all the guests and set up headquarters for several hundred of his thugs in the Brunelleschi Hotel.

James's eyes widen as I relate where we must attack. *I know the place. It's part of the Torre della Pagliazza, one of the remotest buildings within the city walls.*

Zylon jumps off the table in the lobby where we'd just discovered the poker game.

His brothers roar their approval and turn toward James.

This place is quite the luxury hotel with a lot of ancient history. The basement excavations go back to Roman times. James's eyes move to the stairs to the second floor.

The brothers all evolve individually as we climb the stairs. Zeb surprises me by taking the form of a saber-tooth tiger with curved ram-like horns. He bounds up the stairs ahead of us.

Zachary slithers by me. He's now a twenty-foot-long boa constrictor and about half as wide. The crunching sounds his bones make during his final transformation cause my hair to stand up on my neck.

I turn just as Zeno, Zindel, and Zane rip off their clothes and grow to about nine feet. Long hair sprouts all over their bodies, fangs drop, claws extend from arms and legs. Red eyes glow. As they are half demons and half werewolves, I expect them to emit a fowl stink. Instead, they smell like gardenias.

Zohar, Zale, Zander, and Zoltan remain, like James and me, in normal form. Collectively, we will determine what is needed.

Zylon somersaults over us and lands next to Zeb as they crash into the glass doors of the conference room surprising Fairento during a meeting with whom I assume are his lieutenants.

Zeb, the tiger creature, attacks the first man sitting the most distant from Fairento. Crunching down on the man's head, he snaps it in half.

Shouts fill the room. Cries of anger, curses, and fright surround us as Zylon picks up two others, smashes their heads together, and tosses them against the wall.

Fairento makes a run for a side door as James draws his silver sword and cuts two other thugs in half at the torso.

Gamino's lead henchman halts suddenly and turns. His eyes narrow and turn red. He cocks his head to the side as if listening to an inner voice.

My eyes never leave him. The half of me that is spirit wolf senses Satan is present among us.

Zachary, in snake form, wraps himself around another unfortunate and begins to swallow the man whole from the legs up so that the victim can watch his fate. His cries of terror join those of others being taken down by James and the other brothers, who begin to literally pick up their victims and tear them in half.

What looks like a hundred more armed men rush in through the side door where Fairento pauses. One hands him a submachine gun. Fairento aims at James and hits him in the chest. Assuming he's killed my friend, he turns to take aim at me.

Zoltan, now morphed into a huge black wolf, takes the man down and bites off part of the arm and hand holding his gun.

Fairento screams in pain still trying to fire his gun with his missing hand.

To my surprise, his arm and hand quickly begin to grow back!

Satan inhabits Fairento, I telepathically shout to my comrades. I feel myself transforming into my hybrid vampire demon but am cut short by James who unharmed delivers what should be a fatal blow, severing Fairento's head from his body.

The body falls against the wall, shakes, and begins to regrow its head. *I think this is the most bizarre sight I have ever witnessed in my young life.*

I glance around and see another mobster attempting to shoot James from behind. I leap and rip out his neck. He instantly begins to go into a seizure, his mouth foams, and he's dead before he hits the floor. Once bitten, nothing can save my intended victim from my venom.

As I turn, Zane, Zindel, and Zeno each grab three of our enemies as they try to take aim on me. Their headless bodies gush blood and spray the room, covering those nearby, except James, whose silver blood prevents his body from being penetrated by weapons or his clothing or his person stained by blood or gore.

All the while, Zachary the snake slithers through the room swallowing up one victim after another after squeezing the life out of them. His armor-like skin repels bullets just as James's does.

Whirling back around, I see Fairento, now with a completely reformed head, stagger to his feet.

Four men jump Zylon and try to cut him down with machetes after trying without success to hit James, the brothers, and me. Our vampire-driven quickness outsmarts them each time.

Zylon unhinges his large jaws and bites off the head of each of his attackers with lightning speed.

Fairento begins to hop to the dead body parts, touching them. Oddly, they begin to grow and reform into functioning fighters.

James and the brothers continue to slash and chop them into body parts.

Fairento continues to do Satan's work.

I wonder how Satan could be fighting us even after his agreement with God the Father not to go after vampires.

Fairento pauses, turns to me, and with an evil smile answers my thoughts. *God forgot to*

read the agreement. I promised to not "attack"
vampires. I didn't agree to defend against them.

I realize I have one option I haven't tried. As
Fairento springs from one fallen man to the next, I
make a run for him dodging gunfire and slipping
on blood and gore. Hurtling myself, I land on
Satan's vessel and rip out his neck.

Fairento staggers back, black foam runs
from his mouth, and the red glow from his eyes
dissipates as he collapses to the floor. Black ash
rises from the body and disappears into the ceiling.

Hoping Satan cannot heal his vessel from
my venom, I nudge the body with my nose and
jump back as James expertly begin to chop the
body into small pieces. The brothers join him and
start to rip and tear even the smallest body part to
pieces.

Zeb the tiger and Zachary the boa try to eat
the remaining pieces, but I mentally shout for them
to stop. *My venom in this body may kill you if you*
ingest it!

The two back off and turn to the remaining live unfortunates.

More mobsters rush in and stop in their tracks as they see the piles of body parts, blood, torn flesh, and still alive victims being eaten by a tiger and a boa.

One of them shouts, *Where is Fairento?*

I pick up one of the man's remaining body parts and chomp down on it.

James smiles and nods toward me. *Unfortunately, he's all torn up.*

Backing up, the same man yells, "What the hell are you? Let's get the hell out of here."

Before they can leave, James waves his arm, and the doors slam behind and trap them.

Pulling out their guns, they fire at him as he slowly walks toward them. Bullets bounce off him in every direction. He lifts his large sword over his head and whirls, taking down at least ten of them.

I take off running and circle them, biting legs and hands as I go. They drop like flies.

The brothers take the remaining ones, obviously frozen with fear, rip them apart, and throw their body parts into the mass of gore that now litters the conference room.

Opening the doors, James calls over his shoulder. *Follow me.*

We head up the stairs to the third and fourth floors of the Pagliazza Tower suite looking for others. Finding nothing, we swoop down to the restaurant on the first floor and find it empty. The Osteria Pagliazza on the ground floor also remains deserted.

James and I turn and watch as each transformed brother morphs back to his original form. Bones crack and pop as they revert to their original size and skin.

James scratches his chin. *It's near. I would have thought we would have found Vito Gamino in the tower suite.* He turns to me. *Enzo's visions came to him unexpectedly. Yours seem to appear as forewarnings just as we need them. Can you try and see if you can find Gamino?*

I sit on my haunches and lick my chops. I close my eyes and concentrate. *Nothing.*

We need to find him. James kneels next to me. *Try harder.*

I shake my head. *It doesn't work that way…* Darkness takes me. I see nothing for a moment and realize what it means. *He isn't here.*

In the hotel?

Not in the hotel. Not anywhere in the city.

James stands and looks at his blood-splattered companions. Staring back down at me, he smiles. *Then, we will wait. In the meantime, can you transport us home so these men can get cleaned up?*

I snort. *Again. Something easy.*

INTERLOGUE

Vito Gamino bolts upright from his bed in the Pagliazza Tower suite of the Brunelleschi Hotel. Screams of terror invade his nightmarish sleep. At first thinking they were part of his horrific dream, he soon realizes the uproar is emanating from below.

Leaping from his bed, he sheds off his silk pajamas and hurriedly dresses in jeans and a black, long-sleeved Brunello Cucinelli crew-neck T-shirt, a departure from his usual suit and tie.

The bedroom door to his suite swings open accompanied by a blast of steaming air and rolling fog. Satan, in transformation from red skin, yellow eyes, and horns, emerges from the fog and morphs into the Lucifer Morningstar to which Gamino has become accustomed.

Quickly, Vito. Fairento's body is useless to me now. You'll have to do.

"What do you mean useless?" Gamino takes a step back.

His body's been destroyed. I'll use his soul later. But, for now, I need a physical form to work for me.

"What's happening in the hotel below?" Gamino ignores Satan's previous words intent on the sounds of the battle below.

It's those pesky vampires again. They've killed all your men here. They're after you. Take my hand. We need to go.

Gamino steps forward and cringes at the thought of touching Satan. He slowly reaches out and touches the devil's outstretched hand, and his world goes dark.

CHAPTER FIVE

GAMINO AND SATAN

I sit next to James in front of the crackling fire in Kane's den. Shaking my head, I refocus my eyes and look up at my friend who intently stares at me.

What did you see?

How do you always know when I am consumed by a vision?

James rubs my head, and I close my eyes and enjoy the moment. Yes, I have much to share, but I live in each moment. Would that humanlike creatures could do the same.

His response is brief. *You become still, and your eyes go blank.*

While James is more patient than most, today he appears anxious.

The Z brothers are restless as well and ramble like pin balls around the house. Zylon climbs the stairs and then descends them for no particular reason. Zeno, Zindel, and Zale hang out at the bar downing shots of Gentleman Jack. They periodically pace the room as if they've forgotten where they wanted to go. I can hear Zeb, Zachary, and Zohar in the entertainment center flipping between sports channels and making idle chatter. They appear to have the attention span of three-year-old boys. Zander, Zoltan, and Zane sit in the dining room eating beef ribs and drinking wine. Their appetites look more like compulsion than hunger.

It's near sunset, and Kane and Zandra rest upstairs with Moon Blood while Enzo keeps watch at the door to their sleep chamber.

No one awake appears to know what to do next. I know my vision will spring them into action.

I stand and offer James my hind end, but he takes my petting no further. He leans forward in expectation.

I sit and face him. *Satan took Gamino away from the hotel.*

James's eyes widen. *Do you know where?*

It appears he took him to hell.

James jumps to his feet. *Do you mean he's taken his soul?*

No. I stand and pace in front of the fire. *Just for safekeeping. Gamino begged Lucifer to restore his family.*

Wait. What?

I walk over to James and nudge his hand. *Place your hand on my head. Our connection will allow me to convey their conversation to you. All the others will see through you as well.*

James kneels next to me and places his hand on my head.

I close my eyes. *The visions are often garbled. I only know they are in hell because the air stinks like sulfur and the background is consumed in flames. Gamino conflicts with Satan.*

Reign sends his vision, knowing James sees it with him.

"I did as you asked. Florence is under my control. Restore my family as you promised." Gamino mops his brow with a black silk handkerchief and pushes it into the pocket of his jeans.

"You are not finished. I don't have the outcome I want. Those damn vampires have destroyed half your mob." Lucifer's eyes morph from blue to red to yellow.

"No, they haven't. I have men all through Italy and in America, for that matter. What the hell do you want? The people of the city are totally under government control, and I run it all. What more do you want?" Gamino clenches his fists, and sweat runs down his corpulent neck and drips on his designer T-shirt.

Lucifer whirls, and his face morphs into the horned devil. "I want them all on their knees to me! I want all their souls! I want them to build a place of worship in my name! I want to use them to spread my will throughout Italy!"

Gamino backs up. "And how am I supposed to do that?" The mob leader's expression softens.

Reign interjects his thoughts. *I can see what Gamino isn't telling Lucifer. In his heart, Gamino wants to help the people of Florence. His wife Marina grew up there. She loved the city. Gamino thought if he ruled Florence, he could help them through the aftereffects of the zombie plague ...for her. His intentions weren't all bad. He knew Satan wanted to enslave them as he did Gamino, but he thought he could outsmart the devil and help the people on the sly. He was wrong, and Lucifer knew this all along.*

Then Reign sends the rest of his vision.

"Gamino stops. Sweat beads his face, and his chest heaves. A tear runs down one puffy cheek. "You never intended to restore my family to me, did you?"

Satan's face morphs back to its handsome demeanor. "Don't overreact, Vito. Of course, I will restore them to you when we are finished."

Gamino's eyes become slits of suspicion. "Restore them and then enslave them with the rest of the city's inhabitants, you mean."

Lucifer grins. "Well, they will be just as they were before. They'll just worship me every Sunday

instead of my Father. Why are you
Italians all such religious fanatics to
God anyway? I am more worthy and
will even show up so everyone can
see how beautiful I am."

My vision goes dark, and James removes his hand and sits back down in his overstuffed chair by the fire. He scratches his chin and then runs his hand over his eyes. He sits in quiet meditation until the Z brothers, who have experienced my vision through James, gather around him.

Zeb smacks his fist into the palm of his other hand. *How do we get to hell to attack the bastard?*

James holds up his hand. *I think I know another way.*

What way? Zachary sits in the chair opposite James.

I hope you aren't going to use brains instead of brawn, Zylon interjects.

Not entirely. James looks around at the face of each of us. *Instead of destroying Vito Gamino, we use our knowledge of what he truly desires to stop him from doing Satan's bidding.*

Zachary leans forward in his chair and clasps his large hands in front of him. *Why does Satan need Gamino anyway? Why can't he just make people bend to his will?*

Kane's voice slides through our brains. *He doesn't have the ability to force people to worship him or give up their souls. They must give it of their own free will.* Kane descends the stairs holding Zandra's hand. *God the Father gave all men, women, and creatures free will. Satan must gain control over them by having Gamino's government enforce oppressive laws on them, and then make himself an attractive alternative.*

James and Zachary stand and slightly bow to their makers.

How? Zachary presses for more information.

By offering a way out of oppression, by promising them freedom from it if they make him their icon and worship him and obey his laws.

Zachary moves closer to Kane. *But won't they see that as just jumping from one task master to the next?*

James turns to his hybrid vampire-Lycan kindred. *Not if he offers them a seeming Utopia that will make their lives burden free if they follow him. I'm sure Satan can conjure up numerous ways to tempt his potential flock. I can bet he's salivating at the prospect of having nearly half a million more people at his beck and call. Pulling away that many devoted followers of God would be a feather in his cap.*

Yes, Zandra sighs. *Now that our kind is off-base to him, he's going to wage war on humans who have always been his main target. We noticed Lucifer had no problem getting into the fray with you when you attacked Gamino's men.*

I walk forward and nudge Moon Blood and Enzo as they join us. *He said something about not agreeing to fight back when necessary.*

Kane laughs. *An apparent loophole in his contract with his Father.*

James moves slightly closer to Kane and Zandra. *Without all the work he's had Gamino do in the city, he won't be able to get a foothold. But what if we beat Satan at his own game?*

I saunter over and rub up against James's leg. *Since Gamino is prone to want to help the people of Florence because it's his wife's city, maybe we can restore Vito's family to him and take away the devil's power over him!*

Kane's eyes fasten on mine. *Like mother, like son. A problem solver.* The first blood son rubs Moon Blood's head.

But doesn't Satan already have Gamino's soul? Zachary interjects.

The agreement is null and void if Satan doesn't hold up his end of the agreement. James scratches my head. *If we restore Gamino's family to him first, Satan has no claim on the man's soul.*

Zeb crosses his arms. *And how in the world do we do that?*

I look up at James, and he smiles. We both think the name. *Adam.*

Kane and Zandra laugh aloud. *Exactly.*

∞

I stand by James as he uses his cell phone to call the original vampire.

"Brogio, it is your servant, James. Yes... I know... Of course, I will no longer call myself your servant." My friend looks at the roomful of kindred staring at him. "Yes, I'm calling to ask if we might use Adam's skills for a matter of some urgency." He pauses and listens. "No, that won't be necessary. Apparently, Reign can transport us to you. Yes. He is quite talented. Would now be convenient? Yes. All right. We'll be at your door shortly." He hangs up and looks down at me. *Shall we go?*

Wait! Zeb rushes forward. *Don't you need us?*

Not this time. This will all be on Adam. James places his hand on my head, and I close my eyes and visualize the Nova Scotia wine-estate house. When I open them, we are standing in front of Brogio's door.

Adam swings open the door and rubs his hands together in excitement. His parents are immediately behind him.

Adam grabs my neck, swings his leg over my back, sits astride me, and urges me into the house.

"Adam!" Selene admonishes her son. "Don't treat Reign like that."

The child giggles and slides down off me.

James enters and shuts the door behind him.

Brogio shakes his head. "I'm sorry, Reign. I'm afraid Adam thinks of you as his favorite playmate now."

I snort. *It's of no matter. He's but a gnat on my back.*

Adam, yelling at the top of his lungs, runs through the house. "Magic time."

Brogio offers James a seat, and I settle next to the overstuffed chair that somewhat resembles the furnishings of Kane's home.

Selene sits on the arm of her husband's chair, while Adam continues to run faster and faster around the house. His speed increases to the point of invisibility. "Enough, Adam!" his mother warns. "Come sit with us."

The child freezes mid-run, smiles, and drops to the floor next to his parents' chair.

James spends a few moments filling them all in on what we request and why it is important.

Selene can't hide her surprise. "Do you think Adam has the ability to restore life?"

James takes the glass of wine offered on a silver tray from a black-clad servant. "We wouldn't be here otherwise."

I stare into Adam's violet eyes. *Do you think you can do it?*

"I thought about appealing to R'hllor, the Lord of Light, but I'd have to become a follower to implore his help. I don't feel right about it, though." The child smiles at me and glances at his parents.

Brogio leans forward and places a large hand on his son's shoulder. "How do you know about the Lord of Light?"

Adam smiles. "As your child, I have always had the full range of your knowledge, and that of all your progeny. Kane's high intelligence, as well as yours, Poppa, has expanded the information I can access."

Brogio shakes his head and leans back.

I sense advanced maturity in this child since we were last here.

Adam's violet eyes sparkle at me. *It is you, half spirit-wolf, who has awakened the magic in me. The more I do, the wiser I become. I grow older on the inside while remaining young on the outside.*

I crawl closer to Adam. *You said you thought of using R'hllor but don't feel right about it. You knew about our request before we called?*

Yes, Reign. For whatever reason, I am mentally linked to you now. Because you are linked to James, I am connected to him as well. I experience what you both do.

James shoots up in his seat. *Wait. What?* He raises his eyebrows and looks directly at Brogio and Selene. "Your son just told us that he is directly linked to Reign and me."

Brogio smiles. "Yes, we've known that since your last visit."

"I can't say I'm happy about his ability to experience all the bloodshed the two of you inflicted on the evildoers in Florence, but Adam gave us a blow-by-blow of it." Selene picks up a glass of wine from the tray a servant offers and sips it. The pain in her steel-blue eyes is apparent.

James gives me a questioning stare, and I shake my head. *I had no idea.*

I feel the sadness and then mortification as James thinks of these implications. The horror they had witnessed couldn't be good for the child. James silently vows to lessen the mental stains upon Adam the same way he repels dirt and blood from him and his clothes. The child would have his innocence, or as much as James could give him.

Turning back to Adam, I nudge his arm. *So, what can you do?*

Adam stands and walks to the fireplace. He begins to pace just as I have seen Kane do in the past. I understand from James that Kane copied this habit from Brogio.

Adam sighs and appears to grow taller and older. He looks to be about fifteen years of age, much like I glimpsed him on our last trip here.

I blink, wondering if this is my imagination playing tricks on me.

No, I see it too, James shares.

Brogio and Selene appear oblivious to the child's physical changes.

As he paces, Adam speaks aloud, almost in a stream of consciousness.

"My parents were touched by God's hands through the angels. Through them, I am empowered with angel magic from Seth and Mathias. Therefore, I will draw upon that magic to restore Vito Gamino's family to him. Because I will pray to the angels for their help, the family will return as they were before, just as Gamino wishes." Adam stops pacing and returns to his normal five-year-old size.

Brogio squeezes his wife's hand, stands, and approaches his son. "Adam, I'm not sure it's a good idea to call upon Seth and Mathias. They have done so much for us, and I don't want you to wear out that help and protection for a person who may not be worthy of it."

James stands. "Brogio, if Satan can no longer control Gamino through his desire to regain his family, then we can rid his threat on the people of Florence. If the devil gets a foothold in Florence, he can spread his evil to all of Italy and perhaps to the world. We wouldn't ask this of Adam if it wasn't critical."

Brogio's purple eyes grow darker as he focuses on James's face. "I understand the need. But there are no guarantees that Gamino will be in your pocket once he has what he wants. What if the angels help, this backfires, and they refuse to help in the future for an even greater need?"

Adam steps next to his father and looks up at him. "I can make it so that he will lose his family if he doesn't act out of goodness and in a worthy manner going forward."

Brogio grits his teeth, sighs, and shakes his head in agreement. "All right. If you feel confident."

"I do." He turns to me. "Everyone else, stay here. Reign, you come with me. I can use your magic to enhance my own."

I pad along after him into the laboratory that Brogio built for Kane years ago. It appears this is where Adam now studies his magic. All types of books are open to various spells. Concoctions bubble in beakers, and the acrid smells tickle my nose. I sneeze as I always do in this space.

I sit back on my haunches. *What do you need me to do?*

Nothing. Just be here with me. I can draw upon the spirit wolf in you to strengthen me even more.

Adam makes his way to a large leather chair next to a desk spread with large volumes of open books. He climbs up into it, and the room is silent except for the bubbling beakers. He breathes heavily from his belly and visibly becomes relaxed. He again grows older, now perhaps in his late teens. As he closes his eyes, I see that he is drawing upon his parents' memories of Seth and Mathias, their obvious guardian angels.

Through Adam, I see an immediate vision of a tall white-haired young man dressed in a long white robe. His white wings are spread out, and I think he is the most beautiful man I have ever seen. His strong forehead, nose, and jawline are framed by hair that reaches down to his waist. He is standing in what looks like a field of clouds.

The sound of flapping wings interrupts the silence as the beautiful one is joined by a majestic black horse with mane to his knees and a long tail that drags through the clouds. Black feathers cover all four of his feet, and his wingspan is massive. He settles gently next to the angel.

Adam seems to relax further and meditate. His thoughts surprise me. *Seth and Mathias, please guide and protect me. Come to me so that I might receive your blessing and counsel.* The boy pauses. *Thank you for all you have done for my family and those associated with us. Please… let me call upon you again for your guidance and protection.*

I can feel Adam drawing upon the part of me that is spirit wolf, and I kneel as a gesture of service.

The light in the room grows darker, and then a brilliance brighter than anything I have ever experienced blinds me.

The laboratory falls away and becomes a field of clouds. The two angels await us in the distance.

I dip my nose into my feet and swipe my eyes with a paw. As we move forward toward them, I shake my head and am astounded by the luminescent radiance of the light. I am consumed with bliss.

The brightness finally dims to a bearable intensity, and I dare to look upon these incredible creatures before me.

Adam steps forward. *Thank you for answering my call. I—*

We know. Seth's voice is filled with music, and the hair on my body stands up.

Adam falls to his knees in front of the two spirits. *Do you then know that we do this on behalf of God, because His fallen son once again defies His Father's wishes? Can you give Reign and me the ability to restore Vito Gamino's family to him, but only if he will work for the good of God?*

Adam, miracle son of Brogio and Selene, you are an old soul placed in a child's body. You have a greater purpose—Seth then turns to me—*as does your spirit-wolf companion. This will be revealed in time. For now, we will grant you the magic you seek… but know that you had this ability all on your own, all along. You hold the wizardry of all the greats who have existed before you. Use your power wisely. We will be watching.*

Mathias snorts and walks toward me. His footsteps shake the cloudy meadow, and his voice is deep. *Reign, you and James are part of God's destiny. Wait for further revelations. Tell James that he will soon serve his true Master.*

The light surrounding them both begins to dim. As it fades, the meadow disappears and evolves into the laboratory.

"Wow!" Adam springs from his chair. He has reverted to his child version. "That was awesome." He walks to me and places his hand on my head. I am filled with a power I've never known. My entire body tingles, and then the power seems to collect and settle into my brain.

What just happened? I nudge the boy's arm.

We connected and shared the ability the angels assured me I had. Now you hold it too. You can restore Gamino's family to him if he agrees to do God's bidding instead of Satan's. Adam hugs me. *Come on. Let's go tell everyone.*

∞

After I teleport us home, James releases the fur on my neck as we return to Kane's estate. I had placed our landing just a quarter mile from the house so that we could enjoy a walk through the cypress trees lining either side of the long driveway. It is midday, so only the Z brothers are about.

Zeb rushes to greet us as we enter through the door. *It went well?*

I believe so. I glance up at James. *Adam has empowered me, so let's hope so.*

The next step is to pull Gamino away from Satan and bring him here. Do you think you can do that? James takes the tall glass of human blood that one of Noble's assistants offers him.

The servant sets down a crystal bowl of O Neg for me, and I lap it up quickly and roll over with great pleasure. Stretching after a few minutes, I rise to my feet.

Now you are asking something of great difficulty.

Draw upon the spirit wolf in you.

But I can't guarantee that Satan won't snatch him back.

James finishes his nourishment and sets the glass down on the bar in the den. *I don't think Lucifer will be able to hold you in hell. That would be aggressively going against his agreement to not attack vampires.*

I snort. *Unless he sees it as an invasion of his territory.*

All the brothers gather around us. Zylon speaks first. *Take me with you, Reign. I'll fight him to the death to assure you get away.*

No. I lick the brave warrior's hand. *I appreciate your trying to protect me, but there's no reason to put another of us in harm's way. I'll go. It's my duty.*

Adam's childlike voice winds its way through my mind. *My magic will protect you, Reign.*

Adam, no. James's eyes widen in surprise. *There is no reason for you to endure these horrors.*

There was a pause, then Adam mentally answered, *I've seen worse in the minds of my mother and father.*

James grits his teeth, an emotion I haven't seen him display often. *It does not mean you need to see more.*

What? Zachary questions.

The child truly is linked to both of us. James then explains the mental message we just received from Adam.

James searches his mind, but the child is gone.

Zoltan rubs my head. *I'm glad he can protect you, even from afar.*

Rather than wait for further discussion, I close my eyes and visualize what I think hell must be. When I open them, I am surrounded by fire, the sickening smell of sulfur, and the sounds of a distraught Gamino.

He sits on a block of hardened lava, cursing his misfortune, wiping the sweat from his brow, and sobbing in-between.

I see no signs of Satan. I walk up to Gamino, bump his arm so it lands on my head, and retrieve him from hell.

When I open my eyes, he is screaming and backing away from the hulking Z brothers. "What the hell… where am I… how did I…?" His voice rises to a pitch that hurts, and I flatten my ears.

James marches up to him, grabs him by the arm, and drags and shoves him into one of the chairs by the fireplace. "Sit down and shut up. Reign just pulled you out of hell. Be grateful."

The man's eyes grow round and large. "I don't… who are you?"

Zylon glides forward. "Your worst nightmare, you bastard."

The mob boss cringes slightly and then puts his head in his hands. "Are you worse than Lucifer Morningstar?" His entire body shakes. "Right now,

I just want to join my wife and sons. So, go ahead and kill me. I'm done."

James sits opposite Gamino. "That's why we brought you here, Vito, so that you can be with your family again."

The Mafia leader shakes his head and looks up. He eyes James's large silver sword. "Okay, I'm ready. Do it."

James sighs, seemingly to stall his anger and replace it with patience. "You don't get it. You told Lucifer that your greatest wish was to have your family returned to you. We can do that, but there's a price."

Gamino stares at James suspiciously. "I don't believe you."

I move next to James and grin a wolfy smile at the man.

He pushes back into his chair as if trying to escape from me. His hands shake until he clasps them together. "Look, I've been through more than I want to remember in the past day. No, in the past

three years. Who the hell are you… er…
creatures?" He eyes Zylon.

"We're hybrid vampire Lycans, Vito. The
ones Satan can't pick a fight with." Zylon places a
hand on my neck. "This is Reign. He's part
vampire and part spirit wolf. A miracle of sorts.
First, let us show you what we can do for you.
Then, we'll tell you what you have to do to get it."

I close my eyes and feel Satan's power
pressing down on me. He tries to break through the
magical shield that protects us from him.
Suddenly, Adam's presence grows within me. I
remember how we are stronger together than apart.
I embrace combining my strength with the boy's.
The power in my brain releases and spreads
through my entire body. Together, Adam and I
push Satan to the background. He has no power
here.

Combining my strength with Adam's, I scan
Gamino's mind for images of his family and
project them into reality. I open my eyes and

witness Gamino as he suddenly reaches forward with both hands. Tears stream down his haunted face.

Standing next to us are dim visions of a beautiful blonde woman with two twin boys clinging to her.

"Marina! My boys!" Vito Gamino lunges toward them only to have them disappear. He falls to his knees and turns like a wild animal caged and fighting for freedom. "Monsters! You're meaner than the devil himself."

"We did that to show you we can restore your family to you." James stands and holds out his hand. "But there's a catch."

"There always is." Gamino remains, leaving James with his arm out.

"Instead of doing Satan's bidding, you will do God's work." James leans forward.

"What… what do you mean?" Gamino's brows knit together.

"You will restore Florence to its citizens and help them recover properly from the zombie plague. You'll live there, stop the criminal activity, and work within the government to accomplish all this. You will be under our protection and free of Satan's interference. We can't allow you to carry out his will to take over all of humanity."

Gamino takes a deep breath, wipes his face, and blinks at James several times.

"We know that in your heart, because of the love for your wife, that's what you truly want to do. You may have had a checkered past, but you can atone for it all and have your heart's desire, your family with you, and be free of Satan.

Gamino blinks several more times and looks down at his shaking hands and then back up at James. "I'll do it. You seem to know as much about what I desire as Satan does. How could it be any worse that dealing with Satan? Do I have to help heal Florence before I can have my family back?"

"No." James smiles. "That's the difference between good and evil. We trust in the good of people." He extends his hand to Gamino once more. This time, the man takes it. James helps him up and pats his shoulder, then looks to me.

I feel Adam's presence once more as the miraculous power courses through my body. Our energy combines and grows. Fire-like strength surges through my body. It overwhelms me. My strength matches Adam's. A burst of energy flies out of me and creates a blazing archway in the middle of the room. At first the images of Gamino's three family members is faint, but as it grows stronger, the images take on life. Light dances in circles as the three people emerge into reality. Magical healing consumes them and my own body, and my world goes black.

When I awake, Gamino is holding his family in his arms on the floor. His heart-rending sobs echo throughout the room as his wife and children cling to him in utter joy and disbelief. Even a few of the Z brothers, including Zylon, wipe away a tear or two.

Pulling his family up off the floor, Gamino turns to James and me. "I swear on my family's life that I will restore Florence to what it once was. I pledge my eternal allegiance to all of you."

James stands to his full height. "And we accept your pledge in the name of God the Father, but I need you to know that the power that has restored your family will take them away from you again if you fail to act in good faith. That has been written into the magic that has restored them. Remember that as you move forward."

"Then"—Gamino looks up into James's face—"I will have no fear, for I will never do anything to jeopardize my family."

Adam's power retreats to a small place in my brain. With it, Satan's power dissipates and falls away from us. I know he will return somehow, defy his Father, and figure out a way to fight against us again… but not now… not today.

CHAPTER SIX

WARRIORS ORDAINED

After returning Vito Gamino and his family to Florence with the knowledge that the man would use his power and influence to restore Florence to its once glory and freedom, I return to Kane's estate just in time for a nighttime hunt.

James has taken the time in my absence to discuss all that has happened during their rest with Kane and Zandra.

Satisfied that they only had to be bystanders in this scuffle with Satan, they send us off to enjoy the prey in the woods. Instead of joining us, they opt to partake in a supply of human blood while

Zandra assists Kane with one of his many experiments.

Just outside the estate entryway, the Z brothers rip off their clothing and morph into their wolf forms. Bones crack, faces elongate, claws extend, and they are on the ground on all fours at a dead run within minutes. James, as usual, remains himself. Invincible as he is, he has little need to become something more terrifying. I follow suit. Magical power infuses into my every cell. My hybrid vampire-spirit wolf surges forward. I visualize the stars in space and know that I can touch them. I am like a rocket launching toward them. I dash past everyone, leaving them behind as I outmaneuver them all.

A force I have never felt before propels me ahead. Dodging cypress and maple trees, leaping over fallen trunks, and scattering loose rocks, I take down a large moose at a nearby lake. I howl, and James and the brothers join me. I offer James the jugular, while I latch onto the femoral artery.

He refuses my offer and springs upon two boars rutting in the bushes.

Zylon salivates over the moose's jugular, and I send him a quick agreement. *Go ahead, take it.*

The brave warrior latches on with gusto and together we drain our prey dry.

Zane, Zindel, and Zeno team up with Zohar, Zander, and Zoltan and take down a pair of mountain lions. Zale, Zeb, and Zachary are already at work on another large moose.

I am thankful this nearby forest is teeming with prey.

After taking our nourishment and lounging by the water for a few moments, we all take a quick swim in the lake. We slowly emerge from the water, shake off, and turn at the bright white light behind us.

A thrill rips through my veins as I turn to face it. I feel their presence before I see them.

The bright light blinds me until it fades and reveals Seth and Mathias hovering above the lake and floating toward us through the air.

We all take several steps back. James and the Z brothers then quickly fall to their knees with bowed heads.

I keep my eyes open and watch as the angels make a soft landing onto the shore in front of us.

Seth waves his arm, and the child Adam appears next to me.

The boy reaches out to me and, without touching me, makes my entire body tingle.

James, kneeling next to me, reaches out and grasps my neck, and I feel the instant connection among the three of us.

Rise. Seth motions to James and Zandra's brothers.

God's angels are his warriors. Seth's voice is music.

All of you have always been part of a greater plan. Mathias's deep voice vibrates through my body.

God has chosen the thirteen of you to be his warriors here on Earth to rid the world of evil. Seth glows as he speaks. The angel moves his arm over James, Adam, and me. *James, God, not your vampire maker, Zandra, has given you silver blood which grants you invincibility. You more than define the word, "immortal." You have always served and now have the Master for whom you have always longed. You have the purpose you have sought. You are henceforth "James, the Silver Blood Knight."*

Reign, God has given you visions to forewarn you, magic to move through time and space, and immense wisdom, strength, and speed. Your mother and grandfather have given you a deadly bite with which to protect yourself and those you love. You more than define the word, "immortal." Seth continues to wave his arms. *Henceforth, you are "Heaven's Spirit Wolf."*

Adam, you are destined to grow up and live long to defend good in the world through your magic. With James, Reign, and the Moretti brothers, you will have many adventures and test the magic within you. Mathias and I infuse the desire to fight for good in the world within you, beginning now. Your magic will protect you and others always. You will have more power than any human ever born. You are to use it wisely. Henceforth, you are "Adam, Wizard of the Ages."

Mathias paws at the soft bank of dirt next to the lake. His deep voice is a stark opposite to Seth's light, musical one. *Because the Moretti hybrid vampire Lycans are true warriors who do not desire a peaceful life, we grant that wish. That strength will make you invincible. Henceforth, you are "Heaven's Knights."*

Seth holds out the palm of his hand as a caution. *The hybrid vampire-Lycan brothers can only be hurt through those they love. Be aware of that one flaw. Know that all of you, not just some of you, are vulnerable to harm when you are asked to protect those you love.*

Seth and Mathias take one step forward. *We anoint you God's Warriors. James, Reign, and the Moretti brothers have taken their last blood sustenance. Henceforth, you will not need blood, prey, or food of any kind to nourish and sustain you. Take it if you wish, but your bodies will not require it. Seek out evil and destroy it. Fight for good. Rid the world of corruption. Go forth into battle, God's Warriors.*

Before any of us could ask a question, the angels begin to shimmer and fade, along with Adam.

I think perhaps Adam experienced this as a vision …and appeared to us only as a specter of sorts.

The twelve of us stand together in disbelief.

How will we know what evil we must attack? Zachary formulates the question that has formed in all the brothers' minds.

My visions will guide us. I look up at James.

And the link that Adam, Reign, and I share will aid us as well, James adds. *I think, given the warning, it's time for us to leave this place and the ones we love. If our concern over protecting them can somehow put us and them in harm's way, it is what we must do.*

NO! the brothers collectively scream out.

We can't leave Zandra. Zeb pounds his fist into his hand.

She is safe with Kane and can take of herself. James places a hand on his maker's oldest brother.

That's not it. How will we… We have always been with her. Zeb shakes his head violently.

If we stay, we potentially put her and Kane through more battles and stress… the very things they fought so hard to leave behind them. Don't you see that? James slowly stares, one at a time, into each brother's face. *We have a new master now, a different purpose, and we need to find our own way. Your sister and her husband have earned the life they desire. We need to leave them to it and follow our destiny.*

The ten of them fall silent, shake their heads, and, to my surprise, shed a few tears.

I can feel the tender hearts of these ferocious giants breaking.

I will miss my mother and father, our family, my loved ones, but our destiny must guide us now. I know in my heart it will lead us away from them, forever.

INTERLOGUE

SATAN'S IRE

Satan's rage creates great turmoil in his domain. The molten ground shakes, and fire and lava spew through the air, shooting up through fissures gaping open from the devil's wrath.

God's fallen son screams out his rage. "Those damn vampires! Now I know why I can't destroy them. Father has chosen them, once more, to defeat me."

He stomps the ground so hard that it falls open as he hovers above it. "Let those stinking abominations keep Florence. I will find a way to conquer all of Italy by other means." He stops and closes his eyes. A sinister smile spreads across his fiery face, now red, demonic, and the exact picture that stories depict of him. "They will use magic. Then, why not fight them with my own? But it can't be me…" His smile widens to reveal jagged yellow teeth. "Let's see… I need a powerful magician skilled in necromancy. Perhaps Matisse?"

He throws back his head, and his laughter consumes every nook and cranny of hell. Firecracker-like explosions fill the air and cascade into a pyrotechnic display to rival those at New Year's Eve. Even his demons crouch in fear behind darkened corners, and the screams of the damned match the sounds of the exploding light show.

Satan whispers two words: "A lich."

CHAPTER SEVEN

FAREWELLS

Leave? You want to leave? No. Out of the question. Zandra crosses her arms and squares her jaw. Her eyes glow red with anger as she stares at James, her first hybrid vampire Lycan.

Zeb and her other brothers crowd around her. Zeb hangs his head in shame and avoids looking her in the eye. *We don't want to leave you, sister. We never want to be away from you.*

Kane steps in among the brothers and James and wraps his arms around his wife from behind. *Zandra, I don't want them to leave either, but they have a mission. God has ordained them. They need*

to make their own life, their own place to call
home and to feel safe.

She turns in his arms and stares into his face.
You left Brogio and Selene. I guess being together
isn't as important to you as it is to me.

Hurt floods across Kane's face. *I didn't*
leave them until God gave them another destiny,
one they desired, as He has granted us. He
searches Zandra's face. *God has given our family*
another destiny away from us. They only leave to
protect us and our way of life. You can't be selfish
in this matter, my love.

I weave among the legs surrounding Zandra
and press my body against her. She reaches down
and places her hand momentarily on my head.

She sighs. *I'm sorry. I didn't mean to be*
spiteful. She touches Kane's face, kisses it, and
then turns back to her brothers and James. *Where*
will you go?

James shrugs. *I'm not sure yet.*

Zeb places one of his enormous hands on James's shoulder. *We have a place near Florence. We can use that until we find something better.* He looks around. *It's less comfortable than it is here… We never stayed in one place much… but it's good enough for you, Reign, and all of us.*

Kane smiles and shakes his head. *I have a better idea. I have a home that I lease out to corporations and vacationers just outside of Rome. It's quite pastoral and remote enough to keep prying eyes away from your activities. I call it Castelli Romani. It has 12 bedrooms with adjoining bathrooms, a spacious living area, and is quite luxurious. It even has a library that can be converted into a laboratory when Adam comes to visit. I just finished a long-term lease on it. And—* he turns to Zandra—*it's only three hours away.* He looks down at me standing next to his wife. *Not that we need to worry about distance since Reign is our own transporter.*

The group howls with laughter, and the brothers all shake their heads in agreement.

Does it have a forest or available prey nearby? I lick my chops.

James looks at me with raised eyebrows. *Seth and Mathias said we would no longer need to take prey or blood to exist.*

I snort. *They said we could if we wanted to. I'm a wolf. What do you expect?*

Kane reaches for me and places his hand on my head. *Yes... you will be able to quench your thirst whenever you wish.*

This is a wonderful gift. James bows slightly to Kane. *Are you sure you want to give up the revenue stream?*

Kane grins and slaps James on the shoulder. *One of many, many revenue streams, and a minor one at that. This is a gift I have been planning to give you for a long time now. I think this is the perfect timing.*

At that moment, my parents, who had been sitting quietly next to the fireplace, pad through the crowd over to me. Mother places her neck over mine, and Father licks my face. Their voices mingle in my head. *We knew you were born to us for a reason. You have always been special. We understand you must go, but please promise you will visit when you can.*

I wash both their faces with my rough tongue. *I will always return to you.*

Zandra's brothers voice the same to her.

Then—James glances at Kane and Zandra, and finally at Moon Blood and Enzo—*all that's left to do is gather up what belongings we need and have Reign transport us to our new home.*

Instead, I freeze as a vision fills my mind. I immediately recognize what I'm seeing is happening in real time and share it with my companions.

"You are five years old. I forbid you to leave our home!" Selene crosses

her long slender arms and glares at
Adam.

"What is going on here?" Brogio
emerges from his library and stops
next to his wife and son.

Adam spins around and looks up
at his father. "God the Father has
anointed James, Reign, the Moretti
brothers, and me to be his warriors."

"What?" Brogio's eyes narrow
as he searches his child's face.

Adam takes his father's hand. "I
am to use my magic to help and
protect them. We are to seek out evil,
no matter where it exists, and destroy
it."

"Who told you this?" Selene
places her hand on the boy's
shoulder and turns him toward her.

"The angels Seth and Mathias."

Selene takes a step back.

Brogio jerks his head up and
stares into his wife's eyes. Surprise
is written across his face as he

reaches into his pocket, pulls out his cell phone, and dials. "Kane, it's me." He listens intently. "So, it's true. James gave you the details?" He is again silent. "They are relocating?" He rubs his chin. "I don't know. Adam is asking to go. I'll talk to you later."

Selene reads the despair in her husband's face. Turning to Adam, she kneels in front of him and takes both his hands in hers. "Adam, please. Don't rob us of your childhood, your young years, your presence." Tears streak down her beautiful face. "I don't think I can bear losing you, waiting to know each and every day if you are safe from harm. You are just a little boy."

Adam steps back, and Brogio wraps his arms around his son, picks him up, and holds him close. "I knew this would happen."

The boy leans back and
examines his father's face. "Reign
and I were born for this purpose. It's
our destiny. You've always said we
are miracles… We are God's
miracles… here to fulfill a planned
path."

Selene stands and tries to steady
her shaking body. Heartbreaking
sobs wrack her body.

Brogio sets the boy on the floor,
goes to his wife, and takes her in his
arms.

Adam watches them silently. He
strokes his chin, much like his father,
and goes to them. "What if I can
remain with you until I grow up,
until I am eighteen? Would that
help? Would you agree to let me go
then?"

His parents turn to him. "You
would agree to that?" Brogio asks.
"Wouldn't that disobey God's
command?"

Adam sighs. "What if I can satisfy everyone's needs?"

"How?" Selene wipes her eyes and cocks her head at the child.

Adam closes his eyes, hums and chants, spins and shakes, and the room remains silent and warmer than usual. His indistinguishable chanting grows louder, and he spins faster. Slowly, an exact replica of the boy begins to shimmer and glow next to him. Adam continues to spin; his chanting becomes so loud that Brogio and Selene grab their ears in obvious pain. The replicant's shimmering slowly steadies.

As the replicant steps into the here and now, Brogio and Selene can't believe their eyes. Adam's identical twin stands beside him. But, then, something even more amazing occurs. The duplicated blond-haired, purple-eyed boy begins to grow. Already tall for his age at three feet, seven inches, he slowly becomes taller, until he reaches six feet, six inches. As he grows, he matures. No longer a boy but now a young man of about eighteen, his shoulder-length blond hair just touches his broad shoulders and frames a strong forehead, nose, and jawline. Built much like his handsome father, he is muscular and strong even at a young age.

Five-year-old Adam takes a step back and gives his creation the once-over. His eyes twinkle, and he claps his hands together. "There! He has been endowed with everything that I will become, and all my magic. This replicant of me will go with James and his warriors. I will remain here as your child until I am eighteen and can replace this duplicate." He turns to them. "Will that work?"

Brogio shakes his head and blinks his eyes as if to clear his mind.

Selene stumbles back into one of the large stuffed chairs in the den and sits down hard in it.

They both remain speechless.

Replicant Adam begins to shimmer and glow and soon disappears.

Real Adam giggles and runs into his mother's open arms.

Brogio stares at his young son. "I've seen much over the millennia that I've lived, but nothing has ever shocked me more than this."

∞

Temporarily halted by my vision, James, Kane, Zandra, and her brothers are startled when the front door opens in the entryway, and Adam's replicant walks in.

He gives us all a slight bow, and I pad over to him. He rubs my head, and I feel the same tingling magic that always passes between us when Adam touches me.

So, you are the same as Adam but just his eighteen-year-old version? I rise up on my hind legs and place my front paws on his shoulders.

Yes, exactly. I will go with you whenever you are ready.

The sound of Adam's deeper, grownup voice startles me, and I jump down.

Kane throws back his head and laughs. Zandra shakes her head, and the brothers surround the young man and me and make light of the situation.

Zindel and Zeno punch Adam on his shoulders.

Zane sticks his face almost into the young man's, sniffs, and smirks, *You smell just like him.*

Welcome. Zoltan extends his hand, clasps the replicant's, and shakes it.

The others murmur among themselves.

Damndest thing ever. Zachary scratches his head.

We'll see how he performs when the chips are down. Zylon stares at the replicant with hands on his hips.

Zeb grins. *Clever boy.*

Zohar, Zale, and Zander shrug and mill around him.

James walks through the brothers and to my side next to Adam. He looks down at me with a question in his eyes.

Yes. I sit back on my haunches. *He is simply the older version of the boy. This is good.*

James turns to Kane and Zandra. *We'll gather our things and be on our way. We'll let you know when we arrive and reopen the villa.*

Kane flips a key to James and smiles. *Con I migliori auguri.*

James catches the key flying in the air toward him without looking at it. *Best wishes to you as well.*

∞

As James and the brothers gather their belongings, Adam and I spend time among Kane, Zandra, and my parents. Zandra takes Adam aside and begins to instruct him on the importance of keeping in touch with his parents. He listens patiently but clearly is annoyed.

Between Moon Blood and Enzo, I think they'll lick the fur off my face, and I begin to get irritated.

To break the sadness of their mood, Kane flashes me a mental image of the villa that will be our home so that I can picture it to transport us all correctly. A winding gravel road surrounded by an Italian garden leads up to the house. The outside is quite large and constructed with terracotta brick with a blue-tiled roof and matching blue door.

Terracotta bricks lead from the door down a series of steps with a bubbling fountain as its centerpiece.

A patio shaded under a vine-covered arbor overlooks a simple infinity pool surrounded by grass in the back. A large table with cushioned chairs sits on the patio inviting a meal outside. Hanging plants, flowering vines, and twinkle lights woven through latticework create a cozy place to rest.

The house is heavily surrounded by Tuscan cypress trees. Several exterior buildings include a barn and a stable for horses. Further out, a forest surrounds the property. It's populated with maples, birch, ash, poplars, linden, and oaks, along with firs, cedars, redwoods, and pines.

I lick my chops thinking of the fun I'll have hunting prey for sport.

Want to take a tour of the inside of the villa? Kane offers to keep me occupied.

I sit back on my haunches and give him a wide smile with my mouth open and panting.

Although the exterior façade of the villa is quite rustic, the interior architecture has more of a contemporary feel. Kane's voice is filled with pride.

I close my eyes to visualize everything better as Kane takes me through a telepathic tour of the house. Worn wood beams add warmth to the two-story main space. Clean white plaster walls are accented by a modern steel railing, and, of course, an enormous metal-and-stone fireplace.

The contemporary kitchen features wooden shelves and flat-paneled cabinetry. A huge table that can seat more than twelve people sits in another section of the kitchen. With another contemporary fireplace, it has the feel of a great room.

Upstairs, the multiple bedrooms all feature warm wooden beams and white plaster walls with no baseboards or molding. Each has deep inset windows.

The bathrooms are also clean and contemporary and feature wooden beams and cabinets and huge bathtubs or showers to accommodate all the brothers' bulk.

My tour is interrupted by James's voice in my head. *You'll be able to see it in real time in a few minutes, Reign. Shall we get started?*

I jump to my feet, give my parents, who have never left my side, one last rub on their faces, lick Kane's and Zandra's hands, and Adam's replicant and I join James and the brothers. They each lock arms, and James takes hold of my neck fur. I close my eyes, visualize the villa, and when I open them, we are standing next to the fountain near the front door of our new home.

CHAPTER EIGHT

THE RISE OF THE LICH

The hybrid vampire Lycans and Adam pick out their bedrooms and settle in. The brothers and Adam are just joining James and me in the great room when it happens.

This time it is different than before. Instead of just freezing in place, I collapse on the blue-tile floor and hear everyone yelling my name. Spasms overtake me, the room goes dark, and I spiral into a void of nothingness.

When I open my eyes, I know I am in Rome at the Quirinal Palace, residence of the president of Italy. A man of 78 years of age sits in a chair near a large stone fireplace. The room is opulent, filled with art, and appears to be covered with gold ornaments everywhere.

I can see into the man's soul. He is a corrupt politician. I read his mind. He is Sergio Matisse, and he has used dark magic to become the president of Italy. He strives for more… He wants… immortality.

He stands, and I understand that he is a powerful magician, skilled in necromancy. He is amid a spell, a ritual he has repeated over many years. He holds up an object. It is an amulet. Round in shape, the gold metal object is encrusted with what looks like emeralds and amethysts surrounding a small covered enclosure.

I watch as he places strips of parchment, containing arcane phrases inscribed on each strip, into the amulet's pocket and snaps it shut

The room seems to swirl around him. Voices in my head tell me that the amulet is a phylactery and that Matisse has spent his last twenty years repeating this ritual every night. The words in my head are a language so old that I can't recognize them, and it is Matisse's voice, raspy and sinister, whispering each word.

I feel the man's magical powers that are only matched by his malevolence. Sinking to his knees, he pushes back the sleeve of his robe and places the amulet on his left arm facing his heart. I hear the words "Bind my intellect and soul to this phylactery" repeatedly. Then he murmurs, "Store my soul and my life force here." He taps the amulet.

As he repeats the words, the amulet appears to sink into the skin of his arm. He stands, throws off the long maroon robe he is wearing, and reveals his shriveled nakedness. His words grow louder, and his face and body begin to change as he becomes a creature with skin pulled over a skeletal-like frame. He screams in agony but endures it.

A servant enters the room. He too is old. He keeps his head bowed and never raises his eyes or looks upon Matisse. "Have you succeeded this time, master?"

Matisse lets out a guttural roar. "I am a lich! I am invincible! Immune to any mental attack, poisons, diseases. Magical energy protects me, allows me to lead great masses of lesser, undead warriors."

The servant kneels in front of the lich. "Test me, my lord."

Matisse whirls toward the fireplace, pulls a sword off its display on the wall, and drives it into the servant's heart, killing him.

As the servant dies, the lich reaches for a needle and vial on the table next to his chair. Jabbing the needle into one of the veins in his arm, he draws a vial of blood and immediately injects it into the dead man's jugular.

"You will be the first of my undead warriors. I will create an army of ghouls with supernatural powers. You will take my blood now within you and nightly turn others' dead bodies into my mindless killing machines. They, in turn, will do the same." The lich steps back and watches as the servant's body begins to sluggishly move. Standing unsteasily, it staggers to its feet.

"You will prey on young children and humans, drink their blood, and eat their dead flesh."

The servant weaves on his feet and then straightens. "Yes, sire."

The lich smiles with malevolence. "The beauty of it is that you can only eat humans because you now have RC cells inside your flesh and blood which will power you. Eating your own kind will taste disgusting to you. Consuming normal food will weaken you physically and make you vulnerable to man-made objects like guns, knives, and swords, which will then be able to kill you." His smile widens. "Go now to the Milite Ignoto Cemetery nearby and begin. Bite your wrist and infuse my blood mingled with yours into the mouths of the undead. Each undead body you reanimate has the power to turn others as such."

Even in my vision, my body shakes with fear as it allows me to see into this monster's mind.

The voices of James, Adam, and the brothers seem to call to me from a long distance as I fall into another void. I feel my body moving back to those voices. When I open my eyes, I am on my back on the floor, surrounded by my friends. I blink, flip over, stand, and shake my head.

What happened? Concerned, James wraps his arms around me.

I reveal my vision to my friends as they sit on the floor around me.

So, Adam's young voice enters my mind, *what does this lich want?*

The last insight I received is as dire as what we've experienced with Lucifer Morningstar. I snort my disgust. *Matisse is consumed with evil. His goal is to kill every living being in Italy and to amass all its fortune for himself.*

Everyone stands. James looks from brother to brother and then to Adam and finally me. *It appears we have just been sent our first mission.*

THE END

To discover how God's unorthodox warriors battle this seemingly indestructible new villain, watch for *Reign—The Silver Blood Knight Series, Book 2* in the coming months.

Thank you for reading Reign: The Assault of Lucifer Morningstar

If you enjoyed this book and would like to give back to the author, please consider writing a review! Reviews are a tremendous help for authors. So if you were moved and enjoyed this book enough to write even one sentence of encouragement it would be a huge boon.

https://www.goodreads.com/review/new/55836854 -reign

Want more stories through a dogs eyes? Get a FREE story! Join Carol McKibben's exclusive readers group for a free story, GIVEAWAYS, Advanced reader opportunities and Pre-order notifications!
Join at:

http://eepurl.com/bAuq2b

About Carol McKibben

Carol's love of animals, especially dogs and horses, is obvious in everything she writes. When Carol isn't feeding her horde of canine rescues, she's out riding her beloved Friesian on the plains of Texas. Her love of animals leads her to write through a dog's eyes. Carol's message is clear. "If a dog can love us unconditionally, why can't we do the same with each other?" And, her paranormal stories are often filled with characters that might be the most difficult to love.

Carol's writing career began at 14 years of age when she started telling her stories to Labrador Retrievers, Basset Hounds, and any stray that happened by. It wasn't long before people stopped to have a listen as well. Now, Carol writes for people and speaks to large audiences, dogs included.

Find out when the next book comes out!
Connect with Carol McKibben:

Facebook:
https://www.facebook.com/CarolMckibbenAuthor

Goodreads:
https://www.goodreads.com/author/show/4046806.C
arol_McKibben

Website:
www.carolmckibben.com

Other books by Carol McKibben:

The Snow Blood series:

Snow Blood: Season 1

Snow Blood Season 2

Snow Blood: Season 3

Snow Blood: Season 4

Snow Blood: Season 5

Kane: The First Blood Son (prequel of the Snow Blood series)

The First Blood Son series:

Moon Blood: The First Blood Son series (Book 1)

Moon Blood: The First Blood Son series (Book 2)

Moon Blood: The First Blood Son series (Book 3)

Moon Blood: The First Blood Son series (Book 4)

Moon Blood: The First Blood Son series (Book 5)

Stand alone novels:

Riding Through It

Luke's Tale

We often update our books when readers find grammatical errors. If you have found one, please contact us at stephanie@trollriverpub.com.

Find Other Great Books at <u>Troll River Publications</u>

www.trollriverpub.com